STALKING DEATH

Fargo came closer and closer, the Colt in his hand, until h̶ ̶c̶o̶u̶l̶d̶ ̶b̶a̶r̶e̶l̶y̶ ̶s̶e̶e̶ ̶u̶n̶d̶e̶r̶ the smoking wag̶ ̶ the rock. He rou̶ ̶ ̶ched the small ma̶ ̶ ̶side. Fargo was st̶ ̶ ̶bout to speak whe̶ ̶ from the direction of the sage. Well, that answered one question he had. The man in the sagebrush didn't have a gun on him. Or else he'd be dead already.

But the small man spun about and pointed his rifle up at Fargo.

There was time only for an instantaneous impression of the man's frightened face, the pale skin that marked him as an Easterner, his slicked-down hair parted in the center and his watery eyes unfocused. The long barrel of the rifle wavered as Fargo stared into its two black eyes. And then the stranger pulled the trigger. . . .

BE SURE TO READ THE OTHER THRILLING NOVELS IN THE EXCITING TRAILSMAN SERIES!

THE TRAILSMAN
#195

FORT RAVAGE CONSPIRACY

by

Jon Sharpe

A SIGNET BOOK

SIGNET
Published by the Penguin Group
Penguin Putnam Inc., 375 Hudson Street,
New York, New York 10014, U.S.A.
Penguin Books Ltd, 27 Wrights Lane,
London W8 5TZ, England
Penguin Books Australia Ltd,
Ringwood, Victoria, Australia
Penguin Books Canada Ltd, 10 Alcorn Avenue,
Toronto, Ontario, Canada M4V 3B2
Penguin Books (N.Z.) Ltd, 182-190 Wairau Road,
Auckland 10, New Zealand

Penguin Books Ltd, Registered Offices:
Harmondsworth, Middlesex, England

First published by Signet, an imprint of Dutton Signet,
a member of Penguin Putnam Inc.

First Printing, March, 1998
10 9 8 7 6 5 4 3 2 1

The first chapter of this book previously appeared in *Montana Stage*, the one
hundred ninety-fourth volume in this series.

Ⓡ REGISTERED TRADEMARK—MARCA REGISTRADA

Printed in the United States of America

BOOKS ARE AVAILABLE AT QUANTITY DISCOUNTS WHEN USED TO PROMOTE PRODUCTS
OR SERVICES. FOR INFORMATION PLEASE WRITE TO PREMIUM MARKETING DIVISION,
PENGUIN PUTNAM INC., 375 HUDSON STREET, NEW YORK, NY 10014.

The Trailsman

Beginnings . . . they bend the tree and they mark the man. Skye Fargo was born when he was eighteen. Terror was his midwife, vengeance his first cry. Killing spawned Skye Fargo, ruthless, cold-blooded murder. Out of the acrid smoke of gunpowder still hanging in the air, he rose, cried out a promise never forgotten.

The Trailsman they began to call him all across the West: searcher, scout, hunter, the man who could see where others only looked, his skills for hire but not his soul, the man who lived each day to the fullest, yet trailed each tomorrow. Skye Fargo, the Trailsman, and the seeker who could take the wildness of a land and the wanting of a woman and make them his own.

1860, in the Nevada desert
where an isolated army outpost
is called Fort Ravage
because nobody comes back alive . . .

1

Colonel Benjamin Colfax scanned the six soldiers as they lined up by twos beside their horses inside the huge gate of the adobe fort. The harsh morning light promised a scorching day to come. The soldiers were a motley handful, unshaven, shirttails out, uniforms filthy, and boots caked with dust. Their horses were dull with dirt and sweat and the saddles hadn't been oiled for a long time. To a man, all six soldiers returned his gaze defiantly. And with more than defiance—in their eyes was a secretive hatred, a twisted anger. The colonel knew every single soldier under his command wanted him dead.

"Major Roland, come forward," the colonel called out. He tried to keep the bitterness out of his voice, the anger that all his efforts at discipline had failed. He tried to stay professional and cool. But he knew the soldiers heard his frustration and even took delight in it.

Major Roland moved his horse a step forward and doffed his battered hat insolently, rubbing his sweaty face burned carmine by the sun. The major's gut draped over his belt and his shirt was unbuttoned. A long diagonal scar cut across his hairy stomach, which had given him the nickname Major Scarbelly. Scarbelly didn't bother to salute, but nodded to his superior and then belched. The soldiers exchanged smirks. Colonel Colfax gritted his teeth and ignored the effrontery.

"Major Roland," he snapped. "Call for the mount."

"Prepare to mount," Scarbelly said in a snide voice.

The soldiers didn't wait for the order, but began clambering onto their horses. With a groan, Scarbelly hoisted himself onto his swaybacked chestnut and never bothered to give the official command.

Colonel Benjamin Colfax turned away in disgust. He inserted the toe of his spit-polished boot into his stirrup and swung himself up onto his gleaming gray. He was well aware how he looked in the eyes of his men. He sat tall on his horse, his wool sack coat with its single row of brass eagle buttons and gold epaulets glimmering in the sun, his blond hair and mustache trimmed neatly, the long blue barrels of his pistols burnished to a high sheen. Yes, damn it, he thought. Pride was part of army discipline. Part of what made a fighting force hold together in the bad times.

"You fellows have yourself a good time out there," one of the soldiers milling around inside the fort called out.

"Don't you boys get lost," another added.

Colonel Colfax glanced toward a group of soldiers lounging around and playing cards in the shade of the tall adobe wall that surrounded Fort Ravage. They were as sloppy as the six he was about to lead out on patrol, some of them barefoot and shirtless, their pistols jammed into leather belts. The soldiers would spend the day aimlessly, playing cards, gambling, getting into fights among themselves. A few would keep a desultory lookout from the top of the wall.

It was a helluva way to run a U.S. Army outpost, Colonel Colfax thought. The moment he arrived at Fort Ravage, a month ago, he'd seen that the army discipline had completely broken down. And like any good soldier, his instinct had been to reestablish order. But at every turn he'd been opposed by the general. The general. He gritted his teeth at the thought of him. And very quickly he'd realized discipline was beside the point—he'd had his hands full just staying alive.

The wide wooden gates began to swing slowly open to reveal the shimmering land of rocks and sand and alkali. Far in the distance were a few jagged buttes and then the endless cloudless sky, already fading to white in the gathering heat of the day. The colonel brought his gray around to ride out.

"Go get us some hostiles!" a soldier called out.

"Bring us back a few of them red scalps."

"How 'bout a fresh colonel's scalp?" The voice was close at hand, but spoke in an undertone—the colonel knew it was one of the six men he was about to ride out with. It didn't matter which one. As far as he could tell, every man in Fort Ravage was trying to kill him. But then, he had known that was going to be the case when he took on this assignment. He pretended not to have heard the remark.

"Fall in," Colfax snapped, not waiting for Major Scarbelly to give the order.

A flicker of motion caught his eye and he saw the dim outline of the general standing in the window of the command hut. Out of long habit, Colonel Colfax saluted smartly as he rode past, but the general only watched, slack-eyed, then raised the half-empty bottle of whiskey to his mouth and turned away.

Colonel Colfax rode out of the gate of Fort Ravage, and as he passed beyond the adobe walls, he could feel the vastness of the land take hold of him, its sandy emptiness stretching far to the horizon. Somewhere out in the desert were marauding Paiutes. That's what the general had told him. That's what was written into the official reports sent by courier weekly to army headquarters in Fort Independence. And along with the courier went the colonel's special coded message. So far there had been hardly anything to report. Colonel Colfax hadn't seen a shred of evidence of a Paiute uprising anywhere in the territory. In fact, he hadn't spotted a live Indian during the entire month. Just to break the tedium, Colonel Colfax himself had instituted regular inspection patrols. Every other day he took a small unit out on patrol and he spotted signs of Paiutes in the area—abandoned campfires, game trails, occasional lost arrows stuck in the sands. But wherever the hostiles were, they were keeping well out of sight.

What Colonel Colfax had seen were a lot of mysterious comings and goings in Fort Ravage itself, soldiers disappearing on unexplained five-day inspection details and animated conversations that suddenly halted as soon as he approached. When he'd questioned the general about the so-called inspection details, he'd gotten only stony silence in reply. Colfax was certain that the mysterious inspections were connected to the reason he'd been sent to Fort Ravage. And he wrote that in the special coded reports that he sent back to headquarters with the courier, messages that would seem innocuous to a casual reader. But he was also sure that wherever the soldiers were going had to do with the reason everybody at Fort Ravage seemed intent on killing him. He had no doubt the general was part of it too.

In the past month, they'd tried to get rid of him several times. First were the scorpions that found their way into his boots every morning. One bite and he'd have been paralyzed a few days, two and he'd have been a dead man. But he'd done desert duty before and he'd always been in the habit of shaking out his boots and his clothing before getting dressed each morning. Then the rattlesnake appeared in his bed one night. He'd been lucky it had moved under the covers, stirring just before he slipped into his cot. He had killed it with one blow of his pistol butt, then tossed it out into the yard. Next a heavy crate had fallen off the wall one day as he was walking through the yard, missing him by inches. Then a barrel of gunpowder suddenly blew up as he was taking inventory of the ordnance supplies. That time he'd escaped by pure chance, having accidentally stumbled backward and fallen behind a pile of cannonballs that sheltered him from the blast and the flames. None of these occurrences were accidents. Each one had been intended to kill him. But how much longer would his luck hold out? Long enough for him to find out what he needed to know?

They rode four hours through the deserted land. Today there were no fresh signs of Paiutes. Mile after mile, the scruffy sage gave way to alkali flats, then to broken rocks, then gray sage again. The sun was a white-hot disc in the sky and sweat trickled down the colonel's face.

When they had almost reached the southernmost boundary of the land they were supposed to patrol each day, Colonel Colfax decided to call a halt. He led the way along the edge of a long ridge of red rocks, like the spine of a dragon. Just ahead, the line of rocks came to an end and ahead lay a sun-baked mudflat that became a water hole during the rainy season. The skeletons of a few dead trees rose in the distance. There was a small spot of shade to the side of one of the rocks, large enough to cool a few of the horses at a time. It was as good a place to stop as any.

"Give the order for a halt," said Colfax to Major Scarbelly, "just ahead there." Colfax turned half about in his saddle to look back at the straggling line of soldiers behind him. In answer, Scarbelly slumped down in his saddle and his eyes narrowed as he nodded to his commanding officer.

Colfax didn't like Scarbelly's expression and he felt

a twitch between his shoulder blades as he turned about-face forward again. They might just shoot him in the back. If all the men at Fort Ravage and the general as well wanted him dead, then what was to prevent them from just murdering him right here, right now, in cold blood? They would send word back to army headquarters that the Paiutes did it. And there would be nobody to say different. They didn't even need to make it look like an accident.

Colonel Colfax felt the wariness grow in him as they approached the stopping point. His instincts had always been good. From his many years in command, he'd learned to read men; he could feel what they were thinking. There was something in the air now, a kind of gathering tension, like before a thunderstorm.

"You mean stop right here?" Scarbelly asked laconically. The colonel hesitated for a moment, wondering if he should change his mind and insist they ride on. But that wouldn't make him any safer. No, it was better to be on guard but not let them know it. He nodded. "Company halt," Scarbelly yelled out.

"Quarter hour rest," Colonel Colfax said, dismounting. As the men got down from their horses, opened their canteens, and watered their horses, the colonel busied himself with his horse as he observed them surreptitiously. He saw them nodding to one another, exchanging glances. Scarbelly was smirking. Yeah, this was it. The game was up. Should he ride out now? Or take them all on? He rested his hand on the butt of his pistol and leaned against the flank of his tall gray for a moment, considering his options.

Suddenly, he heard a faint noise. A cry of some kind. From some distance away. Colonel Colfax raised his head and turned it to hear better, listening, listening. Yes, there it was again. He hesitated and then curiosity overcame caution. He stepped out onto the cracked mudflat, listening, following the faint cry. The dry wind carried the sound. Behind him, the men fell silent as they watched him, wondering what was going on. The colonel shaded his eyes and peered through the rising waves of heat, scanning the horizon, the black naked trees that wavered in the distance. He pulled out his small brass telescope and swept the landscape. There. He spotted it.

"My God," he muttered. "My God."

The sight was unbelievable, like something from a nightmare. He wasn't sure he was seeing what he was seeing. He became aware of the men walking up behind him but the danger had dissipated, at least temporarily, as the soldiers gathered uneasily, peering into the distance. The colonel handed the telescope to the soldier who had come up next to him.

"Jesus," the man said when he'd looked through it. Wordlessly, he handed it on. The other soldiers took a look. In one of the distant trees hung some kind of a cage. And in it was the form of a human.

"Hey! Maybe it's one of them Paiutes and we can have us some fun," Scarbelly said, breaking the shocked silence. "Let's go have a look." Several of the men raced toward their horses.

"Wait," said Colonel Colfax in such a commanding voice that the normally rebellious men stopped in their tracks. "It might well be a trap. We're going in on full alert."

And for once the men were cooperative as he gave the orders. Two men stayed far back in a rear guard, rifles at the ready, to watch the rocks in case an ambush came from that direction. Two others rode out toward the tree and took positions far out on either side as lookouts. Major Scarbelly and a recruit named Bucknell rode forward with Colonel Colfax as they crossed the barren flat and approached.

The scene grew more horrible the closer they came—the caged man hanging in the ravaged tree. All around the tree lay slaughtered animals—the remains of a cougar and a bristly peccary that had been hacked apart and staked to the ground. Vultures picked at the bits of tattered skin and the bones. The ragged birds flew up in a dusty scattering of wings at their advance. Strange signs in colored chalks were drawn on the ground around a black firepit.

Colonel Colfax raised his eyes to the square cage made of stout branches lashed together. Inside, the powerfully built man stood stripped to the waist, his face and body and dark hair smeared with what looked like dried blood and dirt. He was bearded, not a Paiute. His eyes were wild and his hands were bound behind him and to a bar of the cage to hold him half upright. His lips were cracked and bleeding.

"Wa—ter," the man rasped. "Give—me." Colonel Colfax glanced around behind him and got the all-clear signal from the distant lookouts.

"Private Bucknell. Get the man some water," Colfax commanded. The private rode forward until he came up to the cage which hung a good five feet off the ground. Bucknell seemed confused about what to do. "Stand on your saddle and cut his hands free. Now," Colfax snapped.

Bucknell did as he was told, sawing through the rawhide that held the man's arms to the cage. The imprisoned man staggered as his hands came free and the cage creaked and swung back and forth. The prisoner rubbed his wrists and then took the canteen that was handed up to him between the wooden bars. He drank long and gratefully, then dashed some of the remaining water over his face and rubbed it.

Colonel Colfax felt a wave of surprise come over him as the grime was washed from the man's face. Astonishment swept through him as he recognized the features.

"*Fargo?*" he called out. "*Skye Fargo?*"

The man in the cage scarcely took notice, but rubbed his face with one hand and signaled impatiently for the private to hand him another canteen.

"Fargo? Skye Fargo? Is that you?" Colonel Colfax called out again.

"Yeah," the man in the cage answered, his voice hoarse. He spoke between gulps of water. "That's my name. Glad you came along. But who the hell are you?"

"Skye Fargo," Scarbelly said under his breath. He spit on the ground. It was clear the major had heard of the famous Trailsman and of his reputation.

"Ben Colfax,"' the colonel answered, surprised his old friend hadn't recognized him. Maybe he'd lost his mind. "You must remember me. Why we—"

"Yeah, I remember," Fargo cut him off dismissively. "I met you up in Wyoming once. Think you can get me out of here now?"

"Sure," said Colfax, surprised at Fargo's curt tone. "Sure, Fargo. But how—who did this to you?" Colfax asked.

"Paiutes. The goddamn Paiutes," Fargo snapped. "Now, just get me out of here."

As Colonel Colfax dismounted and gave the orders for Scarbelly and Private Bucknell to get Fargo free, he couldn't help but feel disappointment at Fargo's coldness, despite the circumstances. They'd spent a lot of time together up on the Wind River and again on the plains of Kansas. They were old friends. Fargo had saved his life once out in the buffalo fields and now—well, now he was returning the favor.

Fargo, with the aid of Bucknell's knife, had managed to saw through the rawhide that lashed several of the bars of the cage, and slipped out of the cage down to the ground. He staggered as he hit the dusty earth. Colonel Colfax swallowed his personal disappointment and adopted a professional tone.

"So, Fargo, you say the Paiutes did this. How many hostiles were there in the band?"

"Twenty braves maybe," said Fargo with a shrug. "I was just passing through taking a shortcut to California and they came on me one night."

"Looks to me like them reds was having a party

here," Scarbelly said, kicking one of the animal carcasses.

"They were making sacrifices," said Fargo. "To their war god. I know their language and I heard them talking. They're about to attack every white in the territory. Those damn Paiute savages. I'd like to wipe out every last one of them for putting me up there in that goddamn cage."

"Yeah, now you're talking," said Scarbelly, rubbing his hands together. "I always said the army ought to scalp those reds alive."

"That's right," said Fargo. "Get us some scalps. And I know just where those Paiutes are hiding out. I've seen their trails. I know where their camps are. I say they should just be wiped out once and for all."

Colonel Colfax turned away in confusion. This wasn't the Skye Fargo he'd remembered. What was going on here? And why had the Paiutes put Fargo in that cage anyway?

"You oughtta come back to Fort Ravage and meet our general," Scarbelly said, slapping Fargo on the back. "Why, you and he'd have a lot to talk about. With you knowing where those reds are hiding out, I bet you'd be a real useful man to the general."

"That's enough," Colonel Colfax snapped. He'd heard how the general thought the United States should solve the "Indian problem." He'd heard plenty of people talk that way, including a lot of army men. But wanton killing wasn't official army policy. The official mission of the army was to keep the peace, not incite wars. But now it looked like Skye Fargo himself had gone over to that point of view. He could hardly believe it. He avoided Fargo's gaze and gave the signal for the rest of the soldiers to join them and form up for the return to Fort Ravage. At Colfax's orders, Private Bucknell relinquished his horse to Fargo, supplied him with an extra army shirt from his saddlebag, and doubled up on a horse with one of the other men.

"Fall in," Colfax commanded when they had all assembled. Fargo brought his horse up front alongside the colonel as the rest of the men were drawing up into formation.

"Well, I'm curious to see Fort Ravage," said Fargo to Colfax. "I hear it's a real nice place."

Fort Ravage? A *nice* place? The colonel glanced in surprise at Fargo's face. Fargo winked and flashed him a grin, a grin from the old days when they'd ridden together up in the Windy Range, an expression that no one else in the troop could see. And that told Benjamin Colfax everything he wanted to know and more than he imagined he could hope for. No, Skye Fargo hadn't changed. Somehow, someway, Fargo had come here on purpose. Fargo was playing a game—a dangerous game of life and death.

As they rode back to Fort Ravage, Colonel Benjamin Colfax and Fargo didn't exchange another word except what was absolutely necessary. Instead, they treated one another as chance acquaintances, distant companions. Colfax knew that as soon as they found some time alone, his old friend Fargo would explain what the hell was going on. And in return,

Colfax would tell him what little he'd found out about the doings at Fort Ravage. With every mile, Colfax felt hope rise in him for the first time since taking on this difficult assignment. With two of them, maybe, just maybe . . .

Meanwhile, Fargo rode at his side on the unaccustomed horse. He felt his muscles loosening after having been tied up in the cage for two days. Yeah, it had been a damn sight uncomfortable. His muscles were stiff, his skin burned by the sun, his lips were cracked with dryness—rubbing them with salt had made them worse of course. But it had only been a day since he'd had his last drink of water and he looked worse than he felt. Sure, there'd been some danger in the plan but it had been worth it. The general and the men at Fort Ravage would fall for it. And as he rode along, he thought back on how he got mixed up in this in the first place.

A week before, in the command post of U.S. Army Headquarters at Fort Independence, Three-Star General William McNulty sat behind his desk. His steel blue eyes were steady and only the drumming of his fingers betrayed his anxiousness.

"Thanks for coming to see me," said the general.

"You sent nine armed soldiers. I figured it was a pretty serious invitation," replied Fargo.

"Sorry about that. I'm desperate. And, Fargo, I'm convinced you're the only one who can help me."

"What's it all about?"

"Fort Ravage—worst outpost in the army," explained the general, pushing a map across the table toward Fargo and stabbing his finger down onto the large X marking the fort. Fargo examined the map. Yeah, he'd been across the Nevada desert before and it was just as empty and godforsaken as the map made it look.

"I've heard of Fort Ravage," said Fargo. "A real hellhole."

"We're getting reports from there that the Paiutes are on the warpath, scalping anybody that dares come through. And we lost a couple of wagonloads of settlers heading through there a couple of weeks ago. All slaughtered."

"There's a treaty with the Paiutes," said Fargo thoughtfully. "Wonder why they broke it?"

"Indians are always breaking treaties," General McNulty said. "So does the United States for that matter. It's a rotten system."

"Yeah, but I know some Paiutes," said Fargo. "They've got a chief named Alosaka. A good man, reasonable. Has there been any attempt at negotiating?"

"Ha! Negotiating?" said General McNulty. "These accounts came directly from Fort Ravage." He shoved a stack of reports across the desk. As Fargo perused them, General McNulty poured two glasses of brandy from a decanter. "For the past year there have been people disappearing out there pretty regularly. Drifters, some of them. Soldiers. But we haven't been able to pin it on the Paiutes."

"Well, not until now. According to these reports

there's a regular bloodbath," Fargo said when he looked up. He took a sip of brandy. "They make it sound like Paiutes are killing anything that moves out there. And that Fort Ravage has its hands full just holding them off." He paused a moment in thought. It was funny, he'd been down on the Santa Fe trail and even up into Ute territory in the last month and hadn't heard a word about it. Usually travelers would be talking and certainly the Utes would have known if the tribe to the south had a full-scale war going on with the whites. He sipped the brandy again as his thoughts whirled. "So, who's the commanding officer at Fort Ravage?"

"Pearce."

"General Avery Pearce?" Fargo asked disbelievingly. General McNulty nodded affirmation and Fargo felt confusion. General Avery Pearce was a two-star general, probably the most well-known army man in the country. He'd been instrumental in winning the war with Mexico, and afterward he'd retired to the East, written his memoirs, and went on lecture tours of all the big cities and even to Europe. Why, President Buchanan was always quoting one thing or another that General Pearce had written about duty and honor and patriotism. General Pearce was one of the most famous men in America. But, come to think of it, Fargo hadn't heard anything about him for a few years.

"You're going to ask me why the hell the army sent Pearce out to Fort Ravage," said General McNulty.

"Well, he requested it. Insisted on it just about a year ago."

"So, where do I come in?"

"I . . . I don't think there's an uprising at all," General McNulty said, almost reluctantly. "Even though these reports are signed by Pearce, I . . . I don't trust them. I think there's something wrong out there."

"You think Pearce is trying to stir up a war with the Paiutes? So when does the army start second-guessing a two-star commander?" said Fargo. "You fighting a private battle maybe—general to general?"

McNulty shifted in his seat uncomfortably.

"It's a fair question, Fargo. I'll admit it's hard not to be envious of General Pearce's fame. But no. I've known almost since Pearce got to Fort Ravage that something was amiss. Call it instinct or whatever. So, I sent a man, one of my own, a sergeant, to find out what was happening out there."

"And?"

"Two months later, he got thrown off his horse one day, broken neck." There was a long pause. "The second man I sent lasted six weeks, got shot by a Paiute. The third one caught a fever and died after just a week—or so they reported."

"Could be accidental, bad luck . . ."

"Could be," said the general, sounding unconvinced.

"Did any of the men find out anything before they died?"

"I got a few coded messages slipped into the regular weekly reports," General McNulty replied. "All three men had suspicions. The fort seems to be in chaos. But not one of them could figure out exactly what was going on."

"I don't think this job is for me," said Fargo after a long moment. He downed the last of the brandy and started to rise. "It sounds like an army problem."

"Hold on, Fargo," General McNulty said. "Hear me out. You see, I've got a man there right now. Colonel Benjamin Colfax."

"Ben Colfax? Ben Colfax is at Fort Ravage?" Fargo sat down again. A good man, Colfax—steady nerves, disciplined, honest, fearless. One of the best army men he'd ever met.

"He's been there a month," the general said. "I had two coded messages from him in the first two weeks. There were several attempts on his life already. And then the messages stopped coming." Fargo's eyes narrowed. "No, I don't think he's dead yet," the general answered Fargo's unspoken question.

"But if his messages are being intercepted," Fargo pointed out, "then Ben's in even more danger."

"Right," agreed General McNulty. Fargo could feel the general watching, waiting, hoping, for a decision.

"Fort Ravage is dead center in the middle of nowhere," said Fargo, thinking out loud. "I can't exactly ride up and knock at the front gate. That would look damn suspicious."

General McNulty breathed a deep sigh and Fargo knew the commander had been holding his breath, hoping Fargo would take the job. And now they both knew he was going to.

"No," Fargo said, still thinking. "If they're trying to stir up a war with the Paiutes, then I've got to think of a way to appear to be on the right side of it." And a plan, a strange plan, began to take shape in his mind.

And with the help of three of General McNulty's men, Fargo had sneaked in two nights before and set up everything to look like Paiutes had been there. Then he had himself imprisoned in the cage and hoisted up into the tree. A small skin bag of water was secreted inside his shirt and with it he figured he could hold out for three days. And if the men of Fort Ravage didn't find him by then, McNulty's men would return and supply him with a minimum of food and water. But Colonel Benjamin Colfax had been dependable as clockwork and the plan had worked. It had been damned uncomfortable being tied by rawhide in the cage. And on the afternoon of the first day he'd spotted Paiutes, two on horseback, a quarter mile distant. Luckily, he could speak some of the language the Paiutes used, which was somewhat like the tongue used by the Shoshone, Comanche, and Hopi tribes. But they never came close enough to talk. They'd spotted him, angled toward him to take a look, but didn't stop, maybe figuring it was some kind of white man's business they didn't want to get in the middle of.

And now, a day later, he was riding along with Ben Colfax back to Fort Ravage. He glanced over at the colonel, glad to see him alive. The passing years hadn't changed him much. The tall Missouri-born colonel was still all spit-and-polish, his uniform smoothly fit, his brass buttons gleaming, his blond mustache trimmed perfectly. But Fargo also saw creases in his face, lines that told him Ben Colfax was not at ease, carried a burden. Colfax felt Fargo's gaze on him, glanced over, and nodded with a silent understanding. Yes, there'd be time to talk later.

"Only about ten miles to the fort!" Major Scarbelly called out behind him. "Old Shit Eye is going to be real happy to meet you, Fargo!"

Fargo pulled up until he was cantering alongside Scarbelly.

"Who's this Old Shit Eye?" asked Fargo, feigning innocence. He'd heard the nickname the men used for the famous General Pearce.

"You never heard of General Avery Pearce?" Scarbelly asked in disbelief.

"Sure, I've heard of him," said Fargo. "Always wanted to meet him. You mean to say, *Avery Pearce* is the general at Fort Ravage?"

"Damn right," said Scarbelly. He plucked at one of the chevrons badly sewn onto the sleeve of his dirty army coat. "Why, I've known Old Shit Eye for years. See this here arrow point? Got that down in Mexico under his command. Hell, we stomped those damn Mexicans. Why, I remember the time we was laying siege to a whole garrisoned troop. It was just after the war started and—"

But Fargo's attention was suddenly caught by a gray puff of smoke rising in the sky just ahead, beyond some tumbled rocks.

"Hold up," Fargo called out.

Surprised that a civilian would dare give a command, the army soldiers nevertheless reined in. Fargo pointed to the smoke, which Ben Colfax had just spotted as well. As they watched, the puff became a tall column of billowing black smoke rising into the sky. It was coming from just beyond a short rise studded with boulders.

"What the hell is that?" Colfax wondered aloud.

"Indians. Burning something. Maybe they're having another party. Let's ride right in, right over the top of the hill, surprise 'em, get us some scalps," said Scarbelly, pulling out his pistol and cocking it.

"Paiutes aren't stupid enough to draw so much attention to themselves," said Fargo. "Why don't we fan out and come up on foot, keeping cover behind these rocks in case there's trouble down below?"

"Excellent idea, Fargo," Colonel Colfax agreed immediately. Scarbelly wrinkled his nose at the plan as they all dismounted. "Take my second pistol, Fargo." The colonel handed over his extra gun and additional bullets. Scarbelly glanced suspiciously at Colfax and then at Fargo. He'd obviously caught a tone of familiarity between them. Fargo realized he and Colfax would have to be more careful to give an impression they were almost strangers.

One soldier stayed behind to hold the horses while the rest of the men spread out and ascended the small rocky slope. Fargo ran hunched forward, holding Colfax's long-barreled Colt out before him. The gun was balanced a little differently from his own accustomed

Colt, but he could tell it was a fine weapon, well maintained. He slowed as he neared the top of the rise, then took cover behind a low wall of large rocks and peered over the top. Colfax slid in beside him.

"Not Indians," Colfax muttered as he viewed the scene below.

"Settlers maybe," said Fargo. "But awfully stupid."

It was perfectly clear what had happened. Below was a dry bowl carpeted with shortgrass. There were two men who had been traveling in a carriage drawn by two horses—though how a carriage made for the smooth roads in town ever made it over the rough trails of the Nevada desert, he couldn't imagine. They had stopped and made a campfire which ignited the short, dry yellow grass and spread out of control. Now the carriage and all their belongings had caught on fire. The flames leaped, crackling and snapping. The shorter man was running around in a panic, ineffectually splashing water on the fire from a canteen. Meanwhile, the taller figure had pulled some of their belongings from the fire and was now trying to unhitch the horses from the burning wagon. As they watched, the horses were freed, then panicked, reared, and galloped away, leaving the two stranded. The short one dashed around and around in confused circles.

Fargo's keen eyes scanned the land all around. There was nothing else moving as far as he could see.

"Let's go find out who they are," Fargo said. Colfax gave the signal for the men to move down the hill.

As soon as the short man spotted them approaching, he gave a bloodcurdling yell—but what he yelled, Fargo couldn't make out exactly—and grabbed up a huge pile of rifles from the ground. Then he dove behind a rock. The tall one wearing a wide-brimmed hat ducked down and disappeared into a stand of sage.

"What the hell?" Fargo muttered.

The short man began firing a barrage of bullets. A slug went whining past and ricocheted off a rock. The army men took cover.

"Son of a bitch!" Scarbelly yelled, pulling up his rifle and preparing to shoot.

"Hold your fire!" Colonel Colfax yelled.

"The hell I will," the major shouted. "That little runt almost winged me!" Scarbelly aimed and fired six shots that kicked up fans of dust around the spot where the short man was hiding. Colfax repeated his order and Scarbelly lowered his rifle with a sneer. There was a long silence from down below, then the long rifle barrel reappeared from behind the rock and the little stranger let go another series of wild shots.

"Not too good an aim," Fargo said, ducking back to cover. The man was obviously firing at random. "Why's he shooting at the U.S. Army?"

"Who knows? Maybe he's an outlaw. He'll have to reload of course," Colfax said as they sat behind the rock. "We could just wait him out."

"He's got a pile of rifles though," Fargo said. "That could take all afternoon. I'll go around the long way and sneak up behind him. Keep his attention focused over here."

Fargo left Colfax and his men at the top of the rise and returned to the horses. The he galloped along behind the ridge, keeping out of sight and angling around the small valley. He reined in on the far side, tethered the horse out of sight behind the rise, and ran forward in a crouch as he came into view of the burning wagon. Across the valley, he could see Colfax's men hunkered down as they occasionally popped up from behind rocks to draw the stranger's fire. The black smoke continued to rise up into the sky, although the flames had died down a little. Fargo positioned himself so the smoldering wagon was between himself and the little man crouching behind the rock. So far, he hadn't hit a thing, his aim was so bad. The second man, the taller one, was still hidden somewhere off to the side in a deep stand of sage. Fargo remembered the taller one being unarmed as he dove into the brush, and he hoped he was right.

Fargo came closer and closer, the Colt in his hand, until he could clearly see, under the smoking wagon, the small man lying behind the rock. He rounded the wagon as he watched the small man toss aside a spent rifle, pick up another, and fire wildly up at the hillside. Fargo was standing right over him and was about to speak when a high-pitched yell came from the direction of the sage. Well, that answered one question he had. The man in the sagebrush didn't have a gun on him. Or else he'd be dead already.

But the small man spun about and pointed his rifle up at Fargo. There was only time for an instantaneous impression of the man's frightened face, the pale skin that marked him as an Easterner, his slicked-down hair parted in the center and his watery eyes unfocused. The long barrel of the rifle wavered as Fargo stared into its two black eyes. And then the stranger pulled the trigger.

2

There was a disappointing click. The rifle was empty. The small man's eyes widened in terror as Fargo leaned over and grabbed his collar, hauling him up to his feet.

"That's enough shooting for one day," said Fargo, putting the Colt to the small man's head. "What's your name?"

"Th-th-thaddeus Fleet," the man said. "Just take everything. You can have it all."

"Tell your friend to get himself out of the sagebrush with his hands in the air." Fargo put the Colt to Thaddeus Fleet's temple for extra emphasis.

"Wh-wh-what friend?" said Thaddeus, trembling. His eyes were unfocused and Fargo had the distinct impression he didn't see very clearly.

"Come on down!" Fargo yelled to Colfax and his men. The soldiers began moving down the slope. Thaddeus Fleet squinted in the direction of the hillside and trembled. Fargo cocked the pistol at Fleet's head. "Come on out!" he yelled to the second hidden man.

"Stay where you are!" Thaddeus yelled. The little man's jaw suddenly stuck out as if he'd made a big decision. "Do whatever you want with me. Take anything you want, you bandit."

The soldiers had just come up and Fargo, impatient, pushed Thaddeus Fleet toward one of the men.

"Hold him," he said. He'd have to go in after the second one. Colfax gave orders for several of the men to salvage the remainder of the belongings from the smoking wagon. There wasn't much left. Thaddeus Fleet squinted at the men all around him and shook his head confusedly.

Fargo moved toward the sage, his eyes scanning the gray woolly carpet. The afternoon light lay over the top of the sage and he saw a part of it stir suddenly, knew the second man was hiding there. Colt at the ready, he strode toward the spot. There was a flurry of motion as the stranger realized he was coming and tried to crawl away. He spotted the figure in dark trousers and a wide-brimmed hat, trying to worm under the thick brush.

"Stand up or I'll shoot," he said.

The stranger froze, hesitated, then got up and turned around, head down, jamming the wide hat down low. Fargo grinned to himself. Good try, he thought. But her figure and the shape of her chin and hands gave her away instantly. She was a tall woman, well built and strong, though he couldn't see her face or hair.

"Come on," he said, grabbing her arm and pulling her back toward where Colfax and his men were waiting by the wagon.

35

He found Thaddeus Fleet on all fours, searching for something on the ground, then shouting as he got to his feet, waving a pair of spectacles. The small man wiped the lenses on his shirt, then donned them and looked around, blinking in amazement.

"My God!" Thaddeus Fleet exclaimed. "Why you're . . . you're the army! The United States Army!"

At the sound of his words, the woman Fargo was holding by the arm looked up. He caught a glimpse of her liquid brown eyes, pale skin, and a delicate sprinkle of freckles across her nose. She noticed his attention and hid her face again.

"And just who are you?" Colfax said, stepping toward the small nervous man in the spectacles. Fleet introduced himself.

"I'm a journalist, for the *New York Daily Globe*. I've come all the way from New York City to interview General Avery Pearce."

"Old Shit Eye's too busy for a squirt like you," Scarbelly scoffed.

"That's enough, Major," Colfax said sharply.

"I knowed the general for twenty years and he's not interested in East Coast prissies like you," Scarbelly said, ignoring the colonel. "Besides, he's busy fighting Indians."

"Oh yeah?" countered Fleet provocatively. "Well, I bet he won't be too busy when he sees what I brought him." Fleet gestured toward the woman that Fargo held by the arm and all the men looked. She shifted nervously under their gaze, then slowly raised her head again. A couple of the men whistled when they saw she was a woman.

"Oh, we can get us a little fun this afternoon," Scarbelly said quietly, rubbing his hands together and smacking his lips. Fargo felt the woman stiffen in his grasp.

"Major Roland!" snapped Colonel Colfax. "One more word and you'll do latrine detail for the next year." Scarbelly scowled back at his superior.

"Never mind him," Fargo said to the woman, letting go of her arm. "This is the U.S. Army. Nobody's going to harm you. What's your name?"

She glanced gratefully at him and smiled at the colonel. But before she could open her mouth, Thaddeus Fleet interrupted.

"Who do you think she is? Why, she's Miss Devora Pearce. That's right, the general's daughter!" The troops murmured and craned their necks to get a better look at her. Scarbelly turned purple.

"Well, shit . . . 'Scuse m-m-me, ma'am," Scarbelly stammered, taking off his army cap and crushing it in his hands. "I didn't know who the hell—I mean, heck—I mean, I didn't know you was anybody important."

Devora Pearce didn't acknowledge Major Scarbelly's attempt at an apology but instead drew herself up and addressed Fargo and Colonel Colfax.

"Yes, it's true. I am General Avery Pearce's daughter," she said. Her manner was suddenly self-assured. "Are you men under my father's command?"

"Yes, ma'am," Colfax replied. "We're from the

Thirteenth Mounted Infantry out of Fort Ravage under the able command of General Avery Pearce. I'm Benjamin Colfax," he offered his hand and she shook it gravely, "and this is Skye Fargo."

She took his hand and it was a strong grip, he noticed. But she didn't seem to recognize his name as did most people out West. She pulled off her hat and thick wavy brown hair fell to her waist. Her dark eyes traveled over the dusty and disheveled troop of men who were all trying to stand up straight and looking damned uncomfortable doing it. Scarbelly jammed his hat on his head and sucked in his gut, which gave him a fit of coughing. Fargo noticed that Thaddeus Fleet had pulled a small notebook and a lead pencil from his shirt pocket and was scribbling notes, glancing up occasionally at the men, as if gathering in details. Devora turned her eyes on him.

He himself looked like a sight, Fargo suddenly realized. His lips were cracked with the dryness, his face still streaked with dirt, his hair uncombed, and another man's ill-fitting shirt half buttoned. And a man who's spent two days in the desert sun locked up in a cage smells to high heaven, he thought ruefully. Devora looked them all over and seemed to miss nothing, though her face betrayed none of her thoughts.

"I'm sure you're wondering why I'm dressed like this," she said with a little laugh after a moment.

"Seems obvious to me," Fargo said, shooting a dark look toward Scarbelly, who seemed to be gritting his teeth. If the major's remark about his daughter got back to the general, Fargo was sure he'd be in real hot water. "It's not real safe out here for women."

"The general didn't let me know you were coming for a visit," cut in Colonel Colfax.

"Yes. Well, it's . . . it's a surprise," Devora said with a smile. For a moment, Fargo thought he saw a flash of something cross her face, something like pain, and her thin shoulders sagged for a brief instant as if she were carrying a heavy but invisible burden. "I've come to surprise Papa. He has no idea I'm here. And, uh, how is he?"

This last question was spoken lightly but Fargo could hear the weight and the worry behind her words. Just why was she out in the middle of nowhere risking her life to pay a surprise visit on her father? If she'd wanted, the general would undoubtedly have sent a whole brigade to escort her across the desert. But, no, she'd come alone with this little newspaper man.

"Why the general's fit as a fiddle, Miss Devora," Scarbelly said, trying to ingratiate himself. "Yes, Old Shit Eye—I mean the old man's just as right as rain."

"That's great news," cut in Thaddeus Fleet. He adjusted his wire-rimmed glasses and his words tumbled out as he spoke a mile a minute. "Because my editor wants a whole series of articles all about the general. Going to put my byline on the front page of the *New York Daily Globe*. So, I got to get the general's views on the West and the Indians. And what we're doing out here. This fine country's growing like a weed and the citizens don't know which way it's going. Folks want to know what our greatest American hero, General Avery Pearce, thinks about it all."

"The general ain't going to talk to no lily-livered wimp," muttered Scarbelly.

"Major," warned Colfax again.

"We'd better be getting on to Fort Ravage," Fargo said, noting that the sun had turned warm gold and was sinking toward the horizon. The men busied themselves loading what goods had been salvaged from the burned-out carriage. Two of the soldiers rode off to round up the two animals that had run away and came back with one of them, a swaybacked palomino. As they packed the horses, Fargo made small talk with Devora Pearce and found out that Thaddeus Fleet had contacted her about her father as a preliminary to his interview with the general himself. When she had expressed interest in visiting her father, Thaddeus had offered to take her along.

"We'll have to double up on the horses," Colfax said, interrupting them. Everyone was ready to go. Fargo mounted the unaccustomed horse, missing his black-and-white pinto. Thaddeus was helped onto the swaybacked palomino. The small man scrambled onto the saddle, legs waving in the air. He almost slid off the other side and barely managed to right himself by grabbing the saddle horn. Thaddeus got himself into the saddle but was choking up on the reins. The palomino moved backward a few steps, nervous, skitterish, its eyes flashing white. Feeling the horse moving under him, Thaddeus jerked the reins back hard, the bit cutting into the horse's mouth. The palomino whinnied, then reared up. Thaddeus barely kept his seat as the horse came down hard.

"Let go the reins!" Fargo shouted to the newspaper man. He had to repeat himself twice before Thaddeus Fleet got the idea. But he dropped the reins completely. The palomino was still unsettled, and moved from side to side, threatening to buck or rear again. A horse could always tell when an unskilled rider was on its back. Thaddeus, white as a sheet, sat helplessly on the tall horse. Fargo swung down off his horse and was halfway toward Thaddeus when Devora strode forward. Without a moment's hesitation, she took up the dragging reins and patted the horse's blazed nose.

"There, there," she murmured. The palomino quieted immediately.

"You ever been on a horse?" Fargo asked Thaddeus.

"Not exactly. But it doesn't look real hard. And besides, I can drive a carriage. So I guess I can learn to ride."

"Yeah, well we don't have time right now," Fargo said.

"You ride?" he said to Devora.

"And jump," she said with a nod and a smile in her brown eyes.

"Get down, Thaddeus," Fargo said. The small man slid off and Fargo stood beside the palomino to give Devora an assist. She hardly needed it, but vaulted gracefully into the saddle. She sat easily on the horse, tall and willowy. Her wide hat blew back off her head and hung from its strap while her brown hair floated in the air. Thaddeus Fleet stood nervously wringing his hands.

"My men are carrying most of their gear," the colonel said as he sat on his horse. "Can you take Mr. Fleet?"

"Sure," Fargo said with a note of reluctance. He'd rather have Devora on the saddle behind him. He managed to get Thaddeus up onto his horse and then he mounted. They fell into line. Devora Pearce was riding in front of him and Scarbelly managed to get himself into line alongside her. Colonel Colfax gave the orders for the return ride to Fort Ravage. In a moment they were off, leaving the small bowl of land behind them with the black skeleton of the burned-out carriage.

The vast desert lay in the golden light of the sinking sun. Nubby olive sage and greasewood seemed as if it went on forever, but as they rode mile after mile, the land slowly changed. Dry white patches appeared here and there until they found themselves on a cracked alkali plain. Small buff rocks appeared in the distance and grew bigger as they approached, rose in crinkled towers against the mounded white clouds, and then shrank again behind them and were lost in the distance. Far to the north lay an indistinct line of hills and buttes and the hulking shape sometimes called Dome Mountain. Barely visible beyond were the high peaks with the vestiges of snow from the winter.

As they rode, he had plenty of time to admire Devora Pearce—the curves of her hips, her long flowing hair, as well as her horsemanship. For the first few miles, she rode English style, her back ramrod straight, her knees forward, bouncing up and down with each step of the horse. It was clear the palomino was discomfited by it, shaking its head as if in protest. And Fargo noticed that after a few miles she seemed to understand the horse. She relaxed into the saddle, riding western style. The palomino responded well to her and soon it looked as if rider and horse were long acquainted. Yeah, she was not only a trained horse-woman, but she had good instincts too, he thought to himself. Scarbelly tried to make conversation with her but each time he spoke, she looked off into the other direction and didn't answer.

Thaddeus Fleet sat on the horse behind him, his small arms clutching Fargo's waist.

"So, how far is Fort Ravage?" asked Thaddeus.

"A couple of hours," Fargo answered. "We'll be there just after sunset."

"Are you a recruit or an enlisted man?" Thaddeus said.

"I'm not in the army. I had some trouble—uh, trouble with Paiutes and the colonel rescued me out there."

Thaddeus Fleet's grip tightened at the mention of Indians.

"Savages," Thaddeus said quietly. "Painted devils. I've heard some of them are cannibals. These—what did you call 'em?—Pay-ootes?"

"Paiutes—"

"These Paiutes, are they cannibals?"

"I don't think so," Fargo said. He didn't want to talk to Thaddeus about Indians. On one hand, he didn't want to tell the newspaper reporter a bunch of lies just to make the Paiutes look merely bloodthirsty, but on the other hand, he'd have to convince General Pearce that the Paiutes had been torturing him. He had a role to play after all. The less said, the better.

"You been out West before?" Fargo said.

"Never past the Mississippi," Thaddeus said. "But from what I see, there's a lot of useless land out here. Seems to me people are wasting their time trying to settle this nameless desert."

"It's called Nevada," Fargo pointed out, thinking how Easterners could be so damned provincial, never bothering to find out anything about the rest of the continent. "It's Spanish for snow-clad. And by next year, Nevada might even be a state."

"Well, Nevada or not, I still say it's good for nothing. No reason it ought to be part of the United States."

"What about Comstock?" said Fargo, exasperated. "Last year they discovered that big lode a few hundred miles from here. Gold and silver all mixed together. They say Comstock's going to be the richest mine in the world. That's hardly good for nothing."

"I guess," Thaddeus said, still sounding dubious.

The sun had just set and the peach sky was fading to deep blue when Fargo spotted a dark speck on the wide sage plain. The speck grew and grew until they could see a tattered American flag flying above it. At most army outposts, the flag was lowered precisely at sunset and not a moment after. Fargo guessed this flag was never even taken down. The adobe wall was pitted with bullet holes and the wooden gate seemed to bow outward like it was going to fall.

"*That's* Fort Ravage? That ridiculous pile of mud and sticks is where the army posted the greatest American general in history?" The newspaperman sounded incredulous and angry, and his words poured out of him. "And they gave the general some of the worst-looking soldiers I've ever seen. Why, when I write up this story, there's going to be a national scandal."

Fargo didn't tell Thaddeus that General Pearce had *requested* the post at Fort Ravage. Nor did he remind the journalist that the discipline of the men was ultimately the senior commander's responsibility—and that meant General Avery Pearce. That's the way the army worked—the buck got passed up the ranks and orders and discipline trickled down the other way. And it was a good system as far as it went.

But what had happened here at Fort Ravage? The system had broken down. Or something. Fargo could feel the curiosity tugging at him. A welcoming shout went up from the men doing guard duty on the top of the adobe wall and the gate began to open inward, creaking. Colonel Colfax rode through the gates, followed by Devora Pearce, Scarbelly, and the other men. And as Fargo galloped through the opening in the wall, he wondered what the hell he was going to find inside.

Colonel Colfax shouted out the news that General Pearce was to be informed immediately that his daughter Devora had arrived, along with Skye Fargo. Scarbelly slid down off his horse and started toward the general's quarters.

"And don't forget to tell him I'm here too—Thaddeus Fleet. Just say my name and he'll know me. He's expecting me."

"Sure he is," Scarbelly said sarcastically to Fleet. "I'll let the general know."

Dusk darkened the interior of the fort, but Fargo had an immediate impression of squalor and chaos inside. Men ran around like confused ants, many of them dressed only in filthy long underwear with some vestige of their full uniforms, like a hat or a belt. A group of other men sagged against a wall and appeared to be dead drunk. Several of the horses, kept in a ramshackle corral, caught the excitement and pulled free, stampeding the enclosure. Most of the men pushed forward in a big crowd to catch a glimpse of Devora Pearce.

A loud cheer, mixed with appreciative whistles and catcalls went up as she dismounted. Thaddeus Fleet slid down and pulled his notebook out of his pocket and looking around, began to write furiously. Fargo jumped down and came to stand beside Ben Colfax.

"Worse than I imagined," Fargo said quietly under the roar of the men so that only Colfax would hear. "We'll talk later, first opportunity."

Major Scarbelly appeared at the doorway to the general's quarters and closed it behind him. He eyed the two of them suspiciously. Colfax moved away. They'd have to be extra careful not to be seen talking together. Devora paced impatiently back and forth. The men had quieted and now stood in a circle, watching her like a bunch of starving wolves. Most of the men hadn't seen a woman for at least a year, Fargo guessed.

"Where's my father?" asked Devora, spotting Scarbelly. She flicked her long brown hair over one shoulder. "Take me to him now. Right now."

"Hold on, little lady," Major Scarbelly said, trying to button his shirt over his gut and failing. "The general's said he's real excited you're here. He's just getting himself presentable-like. It will take him a minute."

The adobe building that served as the general's quarters looked as dilapidated from the outside as the rest of the fort. A single glass-paned window had a white curtain drawn across it and the yellow light from an oil lamp flickered inside. Occasionally, Fargo saw a shadow of someone moving inside and expected the general to appear in the doorway. But the minutes passed. Fargo grew impatient too. What could be taking General Avery Pearce so long? His daughter had risked her life and come all the way across the frontier to visit him and he was keeping her waiting?

To keep himself busy, Fargo led his mount to the paddock, unsaddled it, checked its hooves and removed a couple of stones, then gave it a quick comb. Some of the other horses weren't even unsaddled. Out of curiosity, he touched their flanks but none of the other horses were in a sweat. They'd probably been ridden that morning, even the day before, and left standing in their saddles. A good way to ruin horses, he thought. Especially in the heat of the desert. The watering trough was nearly empty. Fargo sighed and spent a few minutes more pumping clear fresh water for the horses, which gathered around eagerly to drink.

Then he rejoined the others. Meanwhile night had fallen and a few torches were lit around the fort. There was only one guard on top of the wall, Fargo noted, and he didn't seem to be keeping a good watch. Some of the men wandered away aimlessly. A dozen or so stood about in idle curiosity. All were still waiting for the appearance of the general. Devora Pearce was having a hard time holding in her temper. She was obviously a woman of high spirits.

"I've had enough of this delay," Devora nearly shouted at Scarbelly. "Colonel, aren't you in charge here?"

Colonel Colfax looked embarrassed.

"Let her pass, Major," Colfax said sternly.

Devora tried to step around Scarbelly to get to the command post, but he blocked her with his huge body. "You heard the colonel. Let me pass."

"Now, I can't do that, little lady," Scarbelly said, taking her arms in his big meaty hands. She tried to shake free from his grasp. "General's orders." She tried to get loose of him, but he only held her tighter, leering.

"Take your hands off her. Now," the colonel said. "Those are *my* orders."

"I'm following the *general's* orders. He said I'm s'posed to stop anybody from going in," Scarbelly said defiantly. "Anybody. That includes the little lady here." Devora struggled in his grasp again. Fargo had had about as much as he could take of Major Scarbelly. He stepped toward the unshaven man.

"Let go of her," Fargo warned. "She won't go in. She'll wait here with us."

"Nah, she's tricky," said Scarbelly. "Her daddy done told me so. Yeah, this little lady is tricky." Fargo wondered if Scarbelly was making things up or if there really was some tension between the general and his daughter.

"I said, let go," repeated Fargo.

"Or what?" Scarbelly laughed. Devora tried to wrench herself free again. It was a difficult situation, Fargo realized as he calculated how he might get Scarbelly to let go without hurting her.

Fargo suddenly feinted a left to Scarbelly's jaw, planning to follow it with a lightning right to spin him about. As he'd planned, the major saw the blow coming. But to Fargo's utter amazement, rather than loosing his hold on Devora, Scarbelly pushed her toward the punch, trying to use her as a shield. It was the instinctual move of a true coward. Fargo's right was easily deflected as he thought up another strategy.

Fargo drew himself up and clasped his hands together, bringing them down with full force on Scarbelly's huge left arm. At the same moment, he moved in and stomped with his full weight, grinding the sharp heel of his boot into Scarbelly's booted foot. There was a satisfying crunch of bone and the major let out a pained yelp and released the general's daughter. She staggered backward and Fargo delivered a whistling right to Scarbelly's jaw that made him reel backward. Scarbelly regained his balance, and his eyes were alight with the kind of fire Fargo had seen before in certain men, the kind of rage that makes them into killers. Scarbelly took a limping step forward and drew his pistol.

Fargo pushed Devora behind him and stared down the barrel of Scarbelly's gun.

"That's quite enough, Major," Colonel Colfax said. "Holster your gun. Now."

But Scarbelly completely ignored his commander and continued to point the pistol straight at Fargo, aiming right between his eyes. Just then the door to the command post opened and the yellow light streamed across the dirt yard. Everyone turned to see General Avery Pearce standing in the doorway. In an instant, the dispute was forgotten. Scarbelly slowly holstered his gun.

The general was an impressive figure, outlined in golden light. His broad forehead spoke of nobility, his oversized head with its famous shoulder-length white mane was carried proudly above powerful shoulders. His tall frame towered above most men. Every American knew about the general's exploits in the war with Mexico. And just about everybody had either heard the general speak on one of his many lecture tours or had read his famous memoir, *My Chronicle of American War*.

General Pearce took a step forward and the light from the torches fell across his face. Fargo saw a ravaged expression, lines etched deep in an expression of bitterness. And he saw the huge protruding brown eyes that gave the general his nickname, Old Shit Eye. The general's eyes had a kind of wariness and a piercing intelligence that seemed to take in everything and everyone at once. Fargo knew he was in the presence of a born leader. Immediately the army troop fell into line without even being asked. But Fargo knew that something was wrong, deeply wrong.

"Father!" Devora threw herself forward and into the general's arms. He hugged her, seemed pleased to see her, then held her at arm's length to look her over.

"Devora, my dear girl!" he said. "How you've grown up. And what a surprise you've given me." He hugged her again. But Fargo heard in the general's words the slight slur of a man who's been drinking. And drinking way too much. Fargo wondered if the long delay was because the general had been trying to get himself sobered up. General Pearce wrapped one arm around his daughter, then looked up expectantly.

"And now, who do we have here?"

"We found this man out in the desert, locked in a cage," Colonel Colfax said, stepping forward and introducing Fargo. Briefly he told what had happened. Fargo saw a look of horror cross Devora's face as she grasped what had happened. Thaddeus Fleet stood scribbling down every word into his notebook.

"So. Skye Fargo himself," General Pearce said, rubbing his chin. "Well, Mr. Fargo, the famous Trailsman. This is an honor. I've heard many stories about you. Out here in the West you're almost as famous as I am. Almost."

Scarbelly guffawed, then fell silent. Devora looked at Fargo with great curiosity. Thaddeus Fleet continued to write down each word the general spoke.

"How did you manage to get that famous, I wonder? And you never even wrote a book about your exploits," the general said.

"Whatever," Fargo said. It was time to win the general's confidence. And one thing he'd gleaned from reading the secret reports that had been sent out of Fort Ravage—the general had developed a real hatred for the Indians.

"Those Paiute savages just about killed me," Fargo said. "And I'll do anything to get my revenge. They blindfolded me and rode me to their village, but I saw where it was. So, I can lead your men there and we can wipe 'em out. Get their scalps. Get rid of that menace once and for all."

"The famous Skye Fargo's turned into an Indian fighter, eh?" the general said, clapping him on the back. Fargo caught a whiff of bourbon, then the odor of coffee. Yes, he'd been right that the general had been drinking. And yet the general was not thoroughly convinced of Fargo's motives. There remained a slight reservation in his voice. "But I've heard you're an Indian friend, Fargo. You speak all those redskin tongues."

"Yeah, I can speak with the Paiutes," admitted Fargo. "And I plan to use that to get my revenge too."

The general's large brown eyes fixed on him as if trying to see into his very soul. Fargo returned the gaze unflinchingly, his poker face unreadable. Their attention was suddenly drawn to Thaddeus Fleet, who stood almost at their elbows, his spectacles glinting in the torchlight. He scribbled into his leather notebook.

"Who the hell are *you*?" General Pearce asked. Thaddeus Fleet jumped at the question and smoothed his center-parted hair. He began to speak with characteristic rapidity.

"Why, I'm Fleet, sir, uh—general. I'm Thaddeus Fleet. Reporter for the *New York Daily Globe*. You know, sir. I'm here to do the interview we agreed on. I wrote to you four times and you wrote back. Maybe you thought I wasn't serious about coming out here to talk to you. And I'm the one who brought you your daughter. That's right. It's because of me that she's here. I brought her to you all the way from the East Coast and let me tell you it's been a right awful journey. But I know our readers are eager to read your thoughts on the American frontier and how Americans ought to be thinking about the history of our great growing nation. Why, you remember I wrote to you how my editor's going to put you on the front page every day. A whole series of articles. I'm sure our readers—"

"You . . . you don't think my public has forgotten me?"

The question seemed startling to Fargo, out of place. The general could have a lot of reactions to the fast-talking New York reporter but that was the last response he'd expected.

"Oh, no, sir," Thaddeus hastened to reassure him. "Why, General, you're every bit as famous now as you ever were. You're the greatest living American hero. Why, my editor is always quoting you. And on the newsroom wall is written that famous thing you always said to your troops down in Mexico: 'A worthy man is paid in kind.' "

General Avery Pearce seemed to blanch at the words. He blinked and a twisted expression, almost like a scowl, passed over his features. But he recovered himself quickly.

"Well, yes, Mr. Fleet. That's just fine. Now, gentlemen, if you'll excuse me, I'd like to visit with my daughter. Colonel?" Ben Colfax came to attention with a smart salute. "Arrange for supper to be served in my office. In an hour. Meanwhile, get our guests settled in." The general, his arm still around Devora, turned to go back inside. He turned back and caught Fargo's eye. "And I'll talk to you later, Mr. Fargo."

The door closed. Fargo stood standing in the darkness of the fort and with the general's departure everything seemed dimmer and somehow more ordinary. Fargo realized what a powerful presence the general possessed. It would be easy to fall under the spell of such a charismatic personality. Such a man could be a great force for good. Or evil.

"Show Mr. Fargo to his quarters," Colfax commanded Private Bucknell. The private nodded and lumbered off with scarcely a backward glance. Fargo hurried to catch up and spotted Scarbelly entering the general's headquarters. It hadn't been the smartest move to antagonize the belligerent major. From now on, he told himself, he'd have to stay out of Scarbelly's way.

They had walked nearly the full length of the adobe longhouse that was built into one long wall of the fort. There were twists and turns where the longhouse followed the wall and they had just rounded a corner away from the central hubbub when Private Bucknell stopped outside a thick wooden door and kicked it open. Inside, Fargo found a small whitewashed room with a wooden floor. In the darkness he could barely make out the interior. The rope-strung cot had no mattress and only a thin stinking blanket folded up at one end. The lamp had no oil. A broken wooden stool lay on one side. Fargo turned around to ask Bucknell where he could get a bath, but the private had disappeared.

It took half an hour to locate the sutler, a fat man who didn't seem to care whether Fargo took supplies or not. He found some lamp oil and another blanket, no cleaner than the first. Fargo also managed to get his hands on a pile of assorted civilian clothes some settler had left behind along with a bar of soap. He stripped down to his shorts and stood in the paddock by the horse trough to get himself cleaned up, then returned to the room, lit the lamp, and dressed. A light tap came on the door.

Fargo opened the door an inch and saw Colfax.

There was no one in sight. Colfax slipped inside the room. They spoke in low voices.

"Sure was surprised to see you, Fargo."

"General McNulty sent me."

"I figured as much. Must have been because of what I wrote about in my last message."

"McNulty only got two messages from you. Right at the beginning. After that, nothing. That's why I came."

"What?" Colonel Colfax sounded very worried. "He didn't get the messages about Dome Mountain?"

"Nope. Maybe your messages are being intercepted."

"They're coded."

"Doesn't matter. They'll still figure out you're in secret communication with army headquarters at Fort Independence. That means you're in even more danger. Tell me what you've found out."

"Well, the general's . . . well, he's strange," Colfax began. "Drinks a lot. Wants to wipe out every Indian on earth."

"There's a lot of that kind in the army," Fargo pointed out.

"Yeah," Colfax agreed. "But McNulty sent me out here because he had a feeling something odd was going on. And he's right. I'm sure you saw the complete lack of discipline. Fort Ravage is a disaster. I started noticing these inspection details. You see, every Monday morning, the general sends twenty men out under heavy marching orders. Very heavy marching orders."

"So?"

"And five days later, they come back, exhausted, marching light. Then on the following Monday, the whole thing happens all over again."

"Let me translate," Fargo said. "You're telling me they leave on Monday loaded with supplies and return on Friday with nothing?"

"That's right."

Fargo thought for a long moment.

"Maybe the general's crooked and he and his men are carting off government property, army supplies, and selling them somewhere. It wouldn't be the first time that kind of thing has happened."

"I thought of that," Colfax replied. "But the men come back tired, dog tired."

"What kind of supplies do they take with them?"

"That's just it. I'm kept away from it all. Loaded wagons come in here on Monday morning and out they go."

"And you can't find out what's inside?"

"Barrels and crates. I asked a few times but I got the distinct message in no uncertain terms that my questions were not welcome."

"And do the same men go every time?"

"They take turns," Colfax replied. "Of course I asked for the assignment when I first became aware of it, but the general just laughed. And I've tried to follow them with my patrol but the men refuse to obey. I didn't want to draw more attention to myself, so I didn't persist. So I haven't even got close to Dome

Mountain." Then Colfax told Fargo about the near accidents that had befallen him.

"I'm glad you're here," Colfax concluded.

"How did you find out about Dome Mountain?" Fargo asked.

"Oh, that was a lucky break," replied Colfax. He was about to go on when Fargo held up his hand for silence. His keen ears caught a whisper of sound outside the door, a crackle of gravel underfoot. Colfax heard it too and raised his head, drew his pistol silently and Fargo signaled that he would head toward the door to surprise whoever was listening in.

"Tell me about the Paiutes around here," Fargo asked, a question designed to keep Colfax talking on. Meanwhile, Fargo crept silently toward the door, grasped the knob in his hand, and suddenly flung it open.

A dark figure stumbled into the room, crying out in surprise.

3

Fargo caught hold of the intruder and pulled him upright. It was Thaddeus Fleet. The small man started to cry out, but Fargo clapped a hand across his mouth and kicked the door shut. Colfax pointed his pistol straight at Thaddeus as Fargo slowly took his hand away.

"So . . . what's going on in here?" the reporter asked in a hushed voice as he straightened his spectacles. "Is this some kind of conspiracy? Huh? Is that it? What's it all about? You guys planning something?"

"How much did you hear?" Colfax asked the little man. He got a shrug in reply.

"Whatever you heard could get both of us killed if it was told to anybody," Fargo said, shaking him by the collar.

"Oh, tosh," replied Thaddeus. "Don't worry about that. I always protect my sources. Is this something to do with why Fort Ravage is such a disaster? Huh? There something big going on here, isn't there? Yeah, I can always just *feel* a story."

Fargo and Colfax exchanged looks. Thaddeus Fleet was not quite as dumb as he first seemed.

"Look," continued Thaddeus in a rush as he pulled out his notebook, "if you two want to talk off the record, I can guarantee your anonymity. And, you know, you can give me the story. The *Daily Globe* will print it as an exclusive. Make you both famous—well, I guess Mr. Fargo's already famous—"

"Let's get one thing straight," Fargo cut in. "We can't tell you what's going down. Not now anyway. And if you breathe a word of this, even about seeing us talking together—" He paused a moment. He didn't want to threaten Thaddeus Fleet. Maybe an appeal—"Look, Thaddeus, this information could get us both killed. Keep your mouth shut for now and we'll give you the whole story as soon as we can. You understand?"

"Sure," the journalist replied. "It's a deal. Your secret's safe with me." Somehow, for all the man's East Coast manner, Fargo felt they could trust Thaddeus Fleet.

"It's time for the general's dinner. We'd better leave separately," Colfax said. He slipped away first, followed by Thaddeus a few minutes later. Fargo waited awhile, blew out the lamp, and walked through the fort toward the general's headquarters.

Night had turned cool as it always did in the desert. There were very few soldiers out and about. Raucous voices came from the mess hall. Fargo walked along the adobe quarters and passed by a window where the curtains were not quite drawn together. Inside he saw Devora sitting at a small table in front of a cracked mirror, brushing her long hair. Even though he couldn't see her face, he could sense from the angle of her body, her isolation. As he watched, Devora laid down the brush and buried her face in her hands. For a moment, he considered tapping on the window, but thought better of it. She deserved some privacy for whatever she was going through. He walked to the door of the general's office and knocked.

It was the strangest dinner Fargo had ever attended.

The general's quarters were a warren of rooms. The walls were literally covered with maps of the territory as well as clippings from newspapers and magazines about the general and his many lecture tours. Dusty shelves were piled with artifacts of all kinds—antique weaponry, Indian totems and fetishes, and even ordinary rocks, sprigs of branches, and pieces of dried cactus. Everything was jumbled together in confusion and every table was piled with papers and books.

In the center of his office, General Pearce had a table set out with four places. Devora entered and offered her hand to Fargo gravely. Her eyes sought his, then lingered on his broad chest, his long, lean frame in a plaid shirt and jeans. The general loudly dismissed Colonel Colfax for the evening with a wave of his hand, then invited Fargo, Thaddeus, and Devora to take their places. Scarbelly brought in the food, which was execrable—stringy beef, half-rotten potatoes, and sour apple sauce. The general downed glass after glass of bourbon but never seemed to get drunk. Fargo and Devora shared a bottle of wine while Thaddeus sipped water. As Scarbelly leaned over the table, he scowled at Fargo and leered at Devora. She blushed, but the general didn't seem to even take notice of Scarbelly's attention to his daughter.

All during dinner, General Pearce kept up a running monologue recounting the war with Mexico, desperate campaigns barely salvaged by his brilliant tactics, battles won by a combination of luck and skill. All the while, Thaddeus Fleet took notes and plied the general with questions, hanging on his every word. Devora sat picking at her food and looking down at her plate, only glancing up from time to time at her father and smiling wanly. Despite the sadness that seemed to hang around her like a dark cloud, Fargo thought, she looked wonderful with her wavy brown hair like a halo around her face and cascading down her back, the curves of her willowy form poured into the snug fit of her blue dress. Deep in the lace at her neckline, he glimpsed the soft valley between her breasts.

". . . and those Mexicans went running with their tails between their legs all the way to the Yucatan," General Pearce said with a laugh. "And that's how we carried the day."

"Well, it's just like you always said, General," Thaddeus Fleet said as he raised a glass of wine in tribute. " 'The worthy man is paid in kind.' "

Fargo saw the general's face wince at the sound of his own famous words and saw Devora's eyes fill with tears. What was going on? The general cleared his throat and quickly launched into another story of military derring-do, while Devora glanced at Fargo and noticed his attention. He slipped his hand under the table and caught her warm soft hand in his own. She didn't pull away, but instead wove her fingers into his, almost as if she were a trusting child seeking comfort. The touch of her fingers was electric and he felt a desire for her quicken his blood. She glanced covertly at him from time to time, with a secret but somehow innocent smile. Go slowly, gently, he told himself. The situation was complicated and dangerous.

During dinner, Fargo had a chance to observe Thaddeus Fleet in action. What he saw modified his first impression of the journalist as a know-nothing Easterner. Thaddeus came across as a pale wimp who couldn't ride a horse. But actually he was as deceptive as a good cardshark. There had been no indication from Thaddeus—by a look or word—that he'd overheard Fargo and Colfax plotting together. Thaddeus spent the whole dinner buttering up the general about his book, his battle victories, his lectures—and General Pearce proved susceptible to compliments, laughing and clapping Thaddeus on the back and calling him a good fellow. Scarbelly didn't like it. As he was serving the food, Scarbelly interrupted Thaddeus a few times as if trying to keep the journalist away from the general. But Pearce would have none of that.

Fargo could see that there was a method to the questions Thaddeus posed to the general. In the midst of accounts of the past battles, the little journalist would occasionally take off his spectacles, wipe them on his shirt, and insert a seemingly innocuous question like why the general was now at Fort Ravage or how many times Paiutes had attacked the fort in the last week. The general deftly ducked all these questions and Thaddeus didn't persist but acted as if he were completely seduced by the general's charm. But Fargo could see that, like himself, Thaddeus had noticed what the general avoided answering.

Finally, the dinner was over. As they rose from the table, and Fargo reluctantly let go of Devora's hand, Scarbelly entered and stood beside the door glaring at Fargo. The general's long snowy hair and golden epaulets glistened in the lamplight.

"I must ask you to leave us now, my dear," the general said to his daughter, kissing her on the forehead. "And you too, Mr. Fleet. I have the weekly report to attend to and I would like to discuss some business with Mr. Fargo. We'll take brandy and cigars in my office. Call in Colonel Colfax," he commanded Scarbelly, "and bring the weekly pouch."

With a soft glance, Devora said a silent good night to Fargo and left the room, followed by Thaddeus. A whiff of her perfume lingered behind. Lavender, maybe.

"Now, come into my office, Mr. Fargo," the general said. "You've been exceedingly quiet during dinner. And you're a man I've often wanted to meet. A man with a reputation like yours is someone I want to know more about. Tell me how you came to be mixed up with these Paiutes?"

As Colfax and Scarbelly arrived and the general poured them all a glass of brandy, Fargo elaborated on the story of his capture by the Paiutes. And he talked about how he would get his revenge, how he would stop at nothing.

"Well, well," the general said, sitting behind his desk. His protruding brown eyes fixed on Fargo for a long moment. Then he seemed to decide something. "This is interesting news indeed. Very timely. I'm going to include this incident in my personal weekly report." The general dictated an account of Fargo's experience, adding many fictional and bloodthirsty details, as Colfax wrote it down. Fargo was careful not to betray his surprise at the general's apparent dissembling and exaggeration. Colfax didn't blink an eye either. Reports to army headquarters were supposed to be accurate, factual. But the general was fabricating and embroidering the story about finding Fargo until it was almost unrecognizable. Fargo suddenly wondered about the veracity of the general's war stories. "How does that sound?" the general concluded.

"It should get headquarters' attention," said Fargo.

"Exactly!" the general said, bringing his fist down on the table. "That's exactly right! They need to snap to attention! And send us some more ordnance. That's *exactly* what we need. Headquarters doesn't seem to realize we're fighting a war out here. A war for the worthy men!" The general began pacing behind his desk, raving, pounding one fist into his palm. "And it's a war we've got to win. The worthy men! Yes, they must be—"

"General Pearce!" Scarbelly suddenly shouted. It seemed to bring the general back to reality. He took a swig of brandy and seemed to regain his composure.

"Now, Major Roland. The weekly requisition report?" Scarbelly handed over a piece of paper which the general scanned, then signed and sealed with wax. It was slipped into the leather pouch that would be sent to Fort Independence in the morning. "Colonel Colfax? Your report?" The general read and signed Colfax's report as well. Fargo knew it was not the secret coded message that the colonel would sneak into the pouch at some point. He watched carefully as the general's personal report was sealed and added to the other reports. Then the bag was tied shut by Scarbelly and the pouch itself sealed, ready for transport. Fargo thought Colfax must be a magician— even though he had been watching carefully he hadn't even seen a possible opportunity for Colfax to slip in his secret message.

The general commanded Scarbelly to take away the pouch and dismissed Colonel Colfax, asking Fargo to remain behind. The whole evening Fargo and Colfax had treated one another as mere acquaintances and they said good night formally. Scarbelly's earlier suspicions seemed to be lulled. As Scarbelly and Colfax left, Fargo thought he could guess how Colfax's secret messages had been discovered. Either Colfax had been noticed slipping it into the pouch or else the general, for some reason, had decided to reopen the pouch after it was sealed and found the message. Now the general poured Fargo another glass of brandy.

"Providence must have sent you to me," General Pearce said grandly, raising a toast. "I have a possible job for you, Trailsman."

"What kind of job?" Fargo said, keeping his voice cool. At last maybe he was going to find out what the general was up to, what these strange goings-on out toward Dome Mountain were all about.

"What if I had a very important shipment—ah, secret army business—to get down to Mexico City in a hurry?"

"That's a tough trip. There's no direct trail. I've been through those mountains many times. You're cutting through the worst kind of desert territory. It's Apache land." He paused a long moment. "But it could be done."

"With four wagons?"

"Wagons? Wagons?" repeated Fargo. "Not on your life. Those mountains are steep. Most of the time you'd be breaking a trail through rugged country and wagons would make it impossible to get through. Whatever you're transporting"—he paused and held up his hand—"and I'm not asking what it is since it's army business—I'd get it packed on burros. They're best in that country. They can't gallop as fast as a horse in the short run, but in the long run they've got more stamina."

"Burros," the general said. "Yes, you're absolutely

67

right. I like the way you think. Good strategy. Will you take the job? Say, five hundred dollars in cash paid at the end of the trail?"

"Sure," Fargo said lightly. Under normal circumstances, five hundred dollars wasn't nearly enough for him to be interested in such a job. And he always insisted on at least half his money up front. But getting himself hired by the general was exactly what he wanted right now. At last he'd get to the bottom of this. "How soon do we leave?"

"Maybe another week," the general said. "Yes, that should be enough time. Meanwhile, enjoy the hospitality of Fort Ravage. Now, if you'll excuse me, I have work to do." General Avery Pearce was pouring himself another glass of brandy as Fargo let himself out.

Fort Ravage was quiet under the flickering stars. There was one man on guard duty. The post was so poorly defended, it was ridiculous. According to the official reports that were going off to headquarters, the Paiutes were attacking almost daily, which of course was a flat-out lie. Fargo walked along the adobe quarters and a movement caught his eye. He spotted the rotund figure of Major Scarbelly hunched over, peeking into Devora's curtained window. Soundlessly, Fargo crept up behind the major and caught a glimpse of Devora Pearce inside the lighted room. She was rolling her stocking down her long, lovely leg. All she wore was a corset that nipped her waist and pushed up her breasts. He glimpsed the darkness between her legs. She unhooked the corset and let it fall to reveal her round breasts, pink-tipped.

Devora stood admiring herself in the mirror, running her hands over her rib cage and breasts. Scarbelly was pressed up against the glass, panting.

Fargo pulled the pistol Colfax had lent him earlier and spun it in his hands, then aimed the butt at the base of the major's skull. The blow was heavy and hard. Scarbelly's head knocked against the glass, then he jerked and sank to his knees, his eyes rolling back. He lay crumpled under the window. Inside, Fargo saw Devora start at the sound and struggle into a silk dressing gown.

Fargo started to inch the window open and at the sound Devora began to call out. Fargo swore.

"It's me, Fargo!" he called out. After a startled instant, Devora came to the window and threw up the sash.

"Why, Skye Fargo! You Peeping Tom!" she said. But he heard a little note of pleasure in her voice. Fargo pointed down and she leaned out of the window to see Scarbelly's unconscious form. She gasped.

"A little advice. Keep your curtains shut," Fargo said.

"Oh . . . oh!"

Her face was inches from his and he pulled her toward him, felt her resist momentarily in surprise, then relax. He tasted the sweetness of her lips as she welcomed his exploring tongue into her mouth.

A soldier shouted, coming their way, probably attracted by her shout. Sure took 'em long enough. He pulled away.

"Just say Scarbelly fainted," Fargo said with a

laugh. He slipped away into the shadows and around the corner just in time. Behind him he heard the babble of men's voices.

"Yes, this man was looking in my window!" Devora said. "Get him away from here."

As Fargo lay on his narrow cot, sleep was a long time coming and his dreams were troubled, filled with images of burning carriages, marching armies, and a woman who looked like Devora trapped in a cage hanging from a barren tree.

He awoke before dawn and dressed quickly. Fort Ravage seemed deserted but the sound of loud snoring came from the bunkhouses. The one man standing guard—he recognized the young Private Bucknell—slumped on the rickety wooden platform beside the fort's entrance, fast asleep. Fargo paused and took a look at the main gate. It had a heavy bolt across the center but was built of warped lumber in such bad repair, with such flimsy hinges, it looked like a strong gust of wind might blow it down. As Fargo began climbing the ladder up to the lookout parapet, the guard awoke with a start. He began to call out an alarm and then recognized Fargo.

"Hot day ahead," Fargo commented as he stood beside Private Bucknell, who was rubbing his eyes as they looked out over the adobe wall.

"Don't feel so hot to me," Bucknell muttered.

Hazy blue shadows of night still hid the land. Dawn's blush was just beginning to show at the horizon and the last stars blazed white in the western sky.

Fargo's keen eyes scoured the flat sage land, looking for what he knew would be there. Then he spotted it. Movement.

"There's something out there," Fargo said. To add emphasis, he drew Colfax's pistol.

"Where?" Bucknell said excitedly. "Maybe it's them Paiutes coming." Fargo saw it again. Distinctly. Yes, all was going according to plan. He pointed toward the spot nearly two miles distant. "I don't see nothing," the private protested.

"Looks like a . . . rider?" Fargo wondered aloud. "No, I think it's just a horse." Suddenly, he gave a low piercing whistle, a sound he knew would carry far to the pinto's sensitive ears.

"What're you doing?" Bucknell said suspiciously. The spot moved against the sage, black and white. Fargo whistled again and Bucknell saw it at last. "Attack! Attack!" he shouted.

"It's just one horse," Fargo said. "No rider. In fact, it's my horse. It must have escaped from the Paiutes who captured me." Bucknell's alarm went unheeded. None of the sleeping soldiers awoke and they watched the approaching pinto. It was a magnificent creature with a broad chest, powerful limbs, and a proud head. There wasn't a finer horse in the West. Fargo opened the gate and the Ovaro came galloping inside, still saddled. Fargo saw that General McNulty's men, who had brought the horse near to the fort under cover of night, had also stuck two Paiute arrows into the saddle for extra effect.

Fargo pulled out the arrows and led the pinto to the

71

paddock. He washed up, changed into his own clothes from his saddlebag, and strapped the knife to his ankle. The trusty Henry rifle was in his saddle and he holstered his Colt, planning to return the borrowed one to Colfax. He began combing and feeding the horse. Getting the Ovaro to Fort Ravage meant he could come and go as he pleased now. And as soon as he could, he'd ride out to check on Dome Mountain. Several men sleepily emerged from the bunkhouse and noticed the Ovaro in the paddock and heard the story from Private Bucknell. Word of the Ovaro's arrival would eventually reach the general too. Nobody seemed suspicious, Fargo saw.

Half the men were already washing up when Private Bucknell remembered to sound reveille. He blew on a battered bugle and the flat notes sounded in the morning air. The rest of the troop emerged from the bunkhouse, scratching their heads and stumbling toward the water pump. They were the sorriest excuse for soldiers that Fargo had ever seen. Why was General Pearce putting up with it? Actually, he realized as he thought over the events of the day before, the general didn't even seem to care or even to notice.

There was no sign of the general. Breakfast was a pile of lousy-looking bacon and foul-smelling coffee. Fargo had some pemmican and dried fruit from his saddlebag instead and decided he would just as soon get going. He mounted the Ovaro and rode toward the front gate.

"Open up! I'm going to have a look around!" Fargo called out to Private Bucknell.

"Can't do that," the private called down. "These gates only open on orders of the commanding officer." Fargo spotted Colonel Colfax emerging from his quarters and shouted to him to come over. Colfax gave the orders and Bucknell scrambled down to open the gate. Just then Major Scarbelly came out of the general's quarters with the leather pouch under his arm. He spotted Colfax and Fargo by the gate.

"What the hell's going on here?" shouted Scarbelly, striding toward them in a rage. "Private Bucknell? What the hell are you doing?" Bucknell paused as he was lifting the bolt from the gate.

"I'm going out to have a look around," Fargo explained. Scarbelly glanced at the pinto questioningly. "Just before dawn the private here spotted my horse wandering outside the fort," Fargo put in as Bucknell puffed out his chest at the flattering falsehood. "It must have broken away since there were two Paiute arrows lodged in the saddle. I'll take it for some exercise."

"Get off that horse, Fargo. No one leaves this post without the general's express permission," Scarbelly said.

"Bullshit," Fargo said. "I'm a private citizen."

"You're on army property," Scarbelly countered.

"Hold on, Major," Colfax snapped. "I gave the order to open the gate for Mr. Fargo. Are you countermanding my order? Are you telling me Fargo's a prisoner here?"

Scarbelly turned around slowly, his eyes narrowed and cold as ice.

"I'm telling you nobody is going anywhere unless General Pearce says so directly. New orders. Straight from the general. As of this morning."

Scarbelly stalked off toward the mess hall and Bucknell climbed back to his lookout spot.

"New orders. As of this morning," Colfax repeated in a low voice to Fargo. They stood near one another but to a casual observer, they wouldn't have appeared to be conversing. Colfax shrugged. "I don't know what it means. Anyhow today's the day the detail returns from Dome Mountain. And the weekly pouch goes out to army headquarters."

"I was watching carefully last night and I still can't figure out how you got your coded message into that pouch," said Fargo.

"I didn't," answered Colfax in surprise. "What was the use? You told me my messages were being intercepted so I didn't bother to put one in."

"But didn't you put one in every pouch?"

"Sure. Until last night. Why—do you think . . . ?"

"Nah. They'll just figure you slipped up or something," Fargo said, trying to keep his voice light. But he could tell from the worry lines in the colonel's face that the same thought had occurred to Colfax that had occurred to him. Fargo returned the Ovaro to the paddock as his thoughts whirled. The general and Scarbelly had been in the habit of opening the mail pouch again after sealing it in Colfax's presence. Only last night the coded message wasn't in there. And that would set them wondering. They might wonder if somebody had got the word back to Colfax that his secret communiqués weren't being received. Or maybe, that Colfax had found another way to send out the coded messages—maybe by a man riding out of the gate in the early morning. Yeah, Fargo didn't like the sound of this one bit.

The bugle sounded assembly and the troops mustered in ragged lines. Colonel Colfax, in his perfect blue wool jacket and shining boots, stood to one side of Major Scarbelly, who wore pants barely held up by suspenders over a dingy Union suit.

"Fall in, men!" Colfax called out. "Count off!"

The door opened and the tall figure of the general appeared, shading his eyes against the morning sun. Devora emerged from behind him, wearing a close-fitting purple dress; she seemed to be looking for someone. When she spotted him, she smiled. The general offered her his arm and they came forward. Thaddeus Fleet came scurrying out of nowhere to stand at the general's elbow.

"Good morning, men of the Thirteenth Mounted Infantry," the general said. He gave a salute and a few of the men returned it. Devora glanced down the rows of unkempt men and Fargo saw she had a hard time keeping the disgust off her face.

"I just received word at dawn that those painted devils are attacking settlers to the west of there. That's right, those Indians are planning a big attack on a wagon train of civilians. So, I need twenty volunteers to ride out and take care of the problem." None of the troop answered, but stood there shuffling their feet.

Fargo's thoughts went around and around. The

general was telling a blatant lie. Fargo had been awake since well before dawn and no messenger had arrived. So what was the general up to?

"I volunteer, General, sir." Fargo was the first to step forward. Devora smiled at him.

Colonel Colfax stepped forward briskly with a smart salute. Reluctantly, a few more men joined in and the general began to point to men he wanted to send. Thaddeus Fleet hesitated a moment, then raised his hand.

"Probably get an exciting story out of it," he mumbled.

"And you'll go too, Major Roland," the general said. "Dismissed!" The men began to dash off toward the paddock, talking excitedly. Fargo had turned to get his pinto when General Pearce called his name.

"Skye Fargo! Fargo! You remain in the fort today. I have many things I want to discuss with you. And you too, Mr. Fleet. You both stay here in safety. The army will take care of this matter."

In fifteen minutes, the men were saddled up and ready to go. Fargo watched with mounting uneasiness as they formed up behind Colonel Colfax. There was no time to wish Ben Colfax luck as the big gate swung open and the troops moved through. Colonel Colfax turned back to salute and Fargo caught his glance. And then they were gone.

It seemed like the longest day of his life. Goddamn, he hated being cooped up. He killed a few hours in the morning riding the Ovaro around the paddock for exercise, then gave it a good, long curry. General Pearce said he'd send for Fargo, but he didn't.

In the late morning, Devora emerged from her quarters, carrying a parasol and seemed relieved to see him. Fargo helped her climb the rickety ladder up to the parapet and they walked around the perimeter of the adobe wall, looking out over the empty land. There was nothing moving, no dust cloud to indicate where the troop was. Devora twirled her parasol and told him how her mother had died when she was young and she had attended boarding schools ever since and rarely saw her father. It sounded like a lonely life. She asked all about his adventures and he recounted some of his travels and escapades—the ones fit for young ladies of course. Several times, their conversation veered toward General Pearce, but it seemed to make her uncomfortable, so they talked of other things. By noon she complained of the heat and went back inside.

The midday meal was slumgullion, the army's idea of meat stew. Just as he finished eating, there was a commotion at the gate. Fargo jumped up with the other men and ran to have a look, hoping to see Colonel Colfax. But instead, it was the detail return-ing from Dome Mountain. The men rode in on empty wagons. And, as Colonel Colfax had said, they ap-peared exhausted, their clothes gritty with dust, faces lined with extreme fatigue. No one seemed to take note of Fargo as he stood among the crowd of men.

"One more week and we'll have enough for everybody!" one of the wagoneers said. A roar went up from the crowd.

"And there ain't one goddamn thing old McNulty can do about it," a voice behind him said. "Old Shit Eye, he's a genius." Fargo turned to see who was speaking and the recruit started, recognizing him. He elbowed the fellow next to him, who alerted the next fellow. In an instant, all eyes were on him and the men fell silent.

"You boys catch any of them damn Paiutes?" Fargo said, as if he hadn't noticed a thing. There was a palpable lessening of tension and one of the men shouted something about getting the skin off an Indian to make himself a rug. The other men laughed and the wagons were taken to the paddock. But the soldiers now watched him covertly and seemed to be guarding what they said whenever he was within earshot. Fargo spotted Thaddeus Fleet off to the side, interviewing one of the soldiers. Later, he'd ask Thaddeus what he was finding out. In the meantime, the day had grown unbearably hot. It was time for siesta. Fargo found himself a shady spot on the parapet against the adobe wall, which caught a little of the afternoon breeze. He rested back and closed his eyes.

Shouts woke him. He came to his feet, fully alert to the tension in the air. The guard at the gate was raising an alarm. Fargo quickly ran around the parapet toward the front gate and saw, in the distance, the return of the troops. In vain, he sought the tall impeccable figure of Colonel Colfax. But as the soldiers drew closer, Fargo saw that Major Scarbelly was in the lead.

The gates swung open. In the rear of the column four horses dragged four travois behind them, loaded with something hidden by blankets. His worst fear had come true.

Fargo climbed down the ladder as the general emerged from his quarters with a half-empty bottle of liquor. He suddenly realized what he was carrying and put it down inside the door, then came forward grandly. Today, inexplicably, the general had donned his dress sword. The silver-and-gold sheath glittered in the harsh light that spilled through the gates and across the dusty ground inside the fort.

Scarbelly slid off his mount and the horses were led away. He hastened to the general's side and they had a hasty whispered conference, during which the general's eyes came to rest idly on Fargo. Scarbelly moved toward the four travois, which were brought into a line. Whatever was strapped on them was hidden by saddle blankets. Fargo knew what was underneath.

"Mr. Fleet!" the general called out, looking around. Thaddeus came forward. "You might want to take note of this for your readers back East. We're fighting a war out here. And this is what it looks like."

In answer, Thaddeus pulled out his notebook and adjusted his wire-rimmed spectacles.

"Engagement with hostiles?" the general asked Scarbelly.

"At least four dozen," the major said. "Just before we got there, they attacked and killed these settlers."

Scarbelly pulled the blanket off the first travois to

reveal the figure of a man in homespun, whose beard and wide felt hat marked him for a farmer. There were four arrows protruding from his chest and belly. The next travois held a young woman, probably the man's wife. Feathered tips of two arrows stuck from her chest. Scarbelly pulled aside the third blanket to reveal two children, also pierced by arrows.

As Fargo expected, the fourth travois held the body of Colonel Benjamin Colfax. Colfax's body was riddled with arrows. But one glance told Fargo what he'd feared most. Before he died, Colfax had been tortured. Tortured for long hours.

4

"Those Paiutes got the colonel," Scarbelly said unnecessarily.

"Pity. What a pity," General Pearce murmured. "You see, Mr. Fleet, how bloodthirsty these savages are. Now write that in your New York city slicker article. Goddamn redskins. Out to kill every damn one of 'em. Wipe 'em off the face of the earth . . ." The general continued muttering to himself.

Devora went pale and pulled away from her father, retreating into the quarters. The general didn't seem to notice she had left; he moved forward and seemed transfixed by the corpses. The soldiers crowded around to get a close look. Fargo stepped forward with them to examine the corpses, trying not to let his emotions show on his face. He noticed Scarbelly watching him carefully, so he checked out the settlers first.

In addition to bloodstains, there was something on the woman's white blouse, he noticed, around the arrow wounds. It looked like black dust. A glance told him that the man's shirt showed the same black dust and he realized what it was. Powder burns. Powder burns from a pistol. The settlers had been shot first—and at close range—then stuck with Paiute arrows. It confirmed what he suspected and the thought of it made him sick. Scarbelly and his men had murdered settlers, innocent people, in cold blood. And he was pretty sure General Avery Pearce had full knowledge of it. And for what? Why? The chilling facts were right in front of him.

Fargo scanned Colfax's body quickly in order not to seem too interested. He took in everything in a swift second, then turned away as he analyzed what he'd seen. Yeah, Colfax had been tortured all right. There were deep slashes carved in his face, one eye was gouged out, and bloodstains on his uniform probably hid other wounds. His skull showed through, ragged patches between the bloody mass where he'd been scalped. At his neck Fargo glimpsed a black spot half hidden by his collar—the colonel had even been burned with a blazing brand. That meant they'd taken their time. Without a doubt, Scarbelly had been trying to get information out of Colfax—like what the coded messages said—or why he hadn't tried to send one the night before. Maybe even what Skye Fargo was doing at Fort Ravage.

Fargo swore silently to himself, a pure black hatred welling up in him. He tried to keep himself under control but all he wanted was to wrap his fingers around Scarbelly's neck and squeeze the life out of the bastard. Or to put a bullet right between the general's two brown eyes.

"Your report, Major Roland?"

"Those redskins were right where you said they'd be," Scarbelly answered. "Only they'd already ambushed that wagon of settlers. We went in full force of course. Surrounded them and killed every one of them. They never had a chance. But we lost the colonel."

Scarbelly didn't even trouble to explain how it was that Colfax's eye was gouged out, which was obvious to everyone. Fargo saw the puzzlement on Thaddeus Fleet's face, until the journalist noticed his gaze and his face became instantly unreadable as he adjusted his spectacles and busied himself by writing in his notebook. Yeah, Thaddeus had put two and two together as well and found it didn't add up.

After a few minutes, General Pearce went back inside his quarters, followed by Scarbelly. Thaddeus Fleet scooted in after them, notebook in hand, talking excitedly.

As he walked across the yard, Fargo found himself shaking with rage, rage at Scarbelly, rage at the soldiers, rage at the general . . . rage at himself for failing to save the life of Benjamin Colfax. It was all he could do to keep from murdering somebody, any one of them, right here, right now. But he would only get himself killed. What he wanted was revenge. Sweet, cold revenge. He climbed up onto the wall and walked around the perimeter a few times to cool off. The troops had covered up the bodies again and dragged the travois into the paddock.

When his rage had hardened into an iron fist

lodged just beside his heart, he began to think more clearly. He could imagine what had happened out there. The troop had found some settlers on the move and butchered them. All to lend credence to the idea the Paiutes were on the rampage. And they had tortured Colonel Colfax, probably to find out about the coded messages. Fargo guessed Colfax hadn't betrayed him, or else he probably already would have been hauled off by Scarbelly and the general, instead of being allowed to roam free in the fort.

Just after sunset, Thaddeus Fleet came out of the general's quarters. He spotted Fargo and headed in his direction.

"Real strange in there," Thaddeus said, closing his notebook and slipping it into his pocket. "General Pearce is drinking like a fish and raving like a lunatic about those Paiutes. Oh, I got some real good quotes. Bloodthirsty quotes. Meanwhile, the major's story about the attack changes every time he tells it. And he keeps ducking the question about how Colonel Colfax got his eye poked out." Thaddeus gave Fargo a sharp look. "You got any theories about that, Fargo? Huh? Want to give me a statement?" Thaddeus reached for his notebook.

"No idea," Fargo said.

"Oh, it's got something to do with what you and the colonel were talking about last night in your quarters," Thaddeus said. "Nasty business. Guess I'd better keep an eye on you."

"Fine," said Fargo. "But just keep your mouth shut, okay?"

He climbed down off the wall and strode toward the paddock. Soldiers were laughing riotously in the mess hall. The four travois stood lined up to one side, still hitched to the horses. This troop took such bad care of its animals, it was a wonder the beasts were still on their feet. Fargo fed and watered the Ovaro and spread some feed out for the other horses and pumped the trough full of water, which no one had bothered to do that day.

Devora's window was dark. For a moment, he hesitated, then knocked on the door of the general's quarters. Scarbelly opened it.

"What do you want, Trailsman?"

"I want to talk to General Pearce."

"Ha! The general will call *you*. If he wants to," Scarbelly scoffed. He added in an undertone, "And watch your back, Trailsman. I'm on to you."

Fargo shrugged and returned to his quarters. He lit the lamp and paced the small room back and forth. There was nothing more he could do here at Fort Ravage, he realized. He'd seen as much as he needed to see. The key was up at Dome Mountain. Somehow he'd have to get out of the fort with the Ovaro and ride up there. Once he found out what was at Dome Mountain, he'd return to Fort Independence and report to General McNulty.

He'd failed to save Colonel Benjamin Colfax. But he wouldn't fail in carrying out their mission, the quest Colfax had died for. But first he had to get out of Fort Ravage. How? The outline of a plan began to take shape in his mind.

He was just about to leave his quarters when he heard a quiet footfall outside and a soft rap on the door. Devora stood there, wrapped in a hooded cloak. She looked terrified. There was no one in sight and Fargo pulled her inside, bolted the door with its flimsy lock behind her, and closed the wooden shutters on the small window.

"What are you doing here?" He kept his voice low.

"Oh, Skye." She clung to him and he felt her chest heaving as if she were trying to keep from crying. "Skye, I'm . . ." She seemed suddenly reluctant to speak.

"It's all right," he murmured. The hood to her cloak fell to her shoulders and her piled-up hair smelled sweet. She was soft in his arms, soft all over. "You're safe here."

"I'm afraid . . . he's gone mad," Devora said. Once she had spoken the word, she seemed to regain control. "Stark raving mad. Insane. I didn't want to admit it to myself. I've been denying it for years. But now I'm sure."

"Crazy? Well, the general drinks a lot," said Fargo.

"And he's drinking more than ever now," Devora said. "But it's more than that. I mean he's lost his reason. I started noticing it a few years ago in his letters. Suddenly there would be a sentence or a whole page of ravings—oh, sure about the Indians. But other things too. And then he'd snap back. I got worried and I told him so. That made him mad at me."

"Did you talk to anybody about it? A doctor maybe?"

"Of course. But the doctor thought I was the crazy one. I mean General Avery Pearce—a *lunatic*? Nobody believed me. And around strangers he could keep himself under control, appear reasonable. At least for a while."

Fargo heard her voice trembling again and knew she was on the verge of hysteria.

"Any man who volunteers to Fort Ravage would have to be crazy. Don't you think?" He smiled grimly and chucked her under the chin. It seemed to work. She smiled back, blinking eyes full of tears. "Get a hold on yourself," he said.

"Yes. Yes. Then Father started making investments. He said he wanted to get rich, only he just ended up giving it to crooks in one get-rich scheme after another. Little by little, he lost all our money and we even had to sell the house. Luckily, the proceeds on his book kept us just barely afloat. I'm glad Mother's not alive to see this." She swallowed hard, then took a breath. "This is awful, isn't it?" she said after a moment. He nodded. "I thought Major Colfax could help, maybe get a medical discharge from the army. But now—" He tightened his arms around her as she shuddered at the memory of Colfax's mutilated body. Devora broke down in sobs and spoke in gasps. "If only—if only I could get Father out of here—away from that Major Roland, that disgusting man. I think Fort Ravage—is just making Father crazier. He talks about insane things and I don't know what to believe. If I could just get him home where I could care for him. I know I could make him better." She looked up at Fargo, her face twisted with pain and fear. "Please help me, Skye. You're my only hope. Help *us*—Father and me."

"You have my promise," he said and saw relief flood her face, felt her soft womanliness pressed against him. He bent over and covered her mouth with his. Her lips were warm and soft as petals. Slowly, he told himself.

Devora's arms were around him, tightly, holding on to him. Did she just want comfort? Or something more? He continued kissing her, exploring her sweetness with his probing tongue. She responded in kind, her tongue darting in, hesitantly, then hungrily. Her hands moved up his back, stroking the broad muscles of his back, and he felt himself grow hard, the blood pounding hot into him.

She felt it too, moaned low in her throat, and pressed against his swelling hardness. He moved his hand upward until his large palm covered the pillowy roundness of her breast.

"Yes, oh, yes, Skye," she whispered in his ear. "Yes, I want you. Please, just make me forget everything. For a while."

In answer, Fargo slipped his hand inside the neckline of her dress and cupped the warmth of her breast, feeling the soft nipple grow firm and hard as a berry. Devora pulled the pins from her hair and it tumbled over her shoulders and down her back. She purred deep in her throat and moved rhythmically against him. She unbuttoned his shirt and he slipped out of it. Her touch was like an electric shock as her fingers lightly brushed his skin, played with his hair, the lobes of his ears. He began unbuttoning her dress as she fumbled with his belt buckle.

"Twenty-five, twenty-six," he counted as he reached the last button, the dress parted and fell to the floor around her. She stepped out of her petticoat and pulled off her panties. She stood in the glow of the lamplight in the corset that outlined her slender waist. The high mounds of her breasts pushed up over the lace. Her legs were clad in silken hose held by slender garters that striped her lean thighs. The dark triangle of fur glistened.

Fargo pulled down his jeans. Devora took in the sight of his massive cock. She shivered and sat down on the edge of the bed. She rolled down her hose and kicked them off, then unhooked the corset and tossed it aside. In the golden radiance, her large breasts shone. Fargo knelt before her, tongued her nipples, buried his head between their softness, then bent to kiss the tops of her thighs.

Shyly, she opened her knees as he nuzzled her, inhaling the warm musk odor that rose from her, gently nipping her tender skin. She shivered. Inch by inch, he worked his way upward. Devora giggled, then sighed as she lay back across the bed. His tongue found the slick folds of her, swollen with desire, his fingers gently playing, exploring, seeking and finding the dark tunnel of her, entering as she groaned and tossed on the bed. He sucked and flicked across the hard knob of her desire.

Devora cried out, then stifled herself, writhing back

and forth. She tasted of honey and musk. Fargo nuzzled his face against her, his tongue a hot probe as her body tightened and she came, the ecstasy wracking her.

"Oh, oh," she cried out softly. Fargo rose and she opened full to him, the wet heat of her drawing him in, the swollen head of his passion at her entrance, pushing, pushing into her slowly, tight and hot throbbing around him as he sank, deeper and deeper between her legs, felt himself all the way inside her, filling her tight heat. He cupped his hands beneath her buttocks and plunged again, driving, slowly, exquisitely slowly, enjoying the sight of her beneath him, the pale smooth mounds of her breasts and the dark brown eyes never leaving his.

"Skye. Yes, let's forget everything. Let's—" He gently covered her mouth with his hand and her eyes smiled up at him as she lightly bit his palm. He kissed her mouth, their tongues entwined as his rod seemed to grow larger, heat flowing through his body, along his spine and all his limbs, pouring into the hard throbbing of his desire. He could feel it gathering at the base of him, the urgent tightening, the pull. He pushed slowly, deeper, feeling the tip deep against her, inside. She shivered and cried out, raised her ankles to hook them around him and he pushed upward, then sideways against her inside, varying the angle until she was panting again almost at the brink and he slowly, slowly brought her over again, watched as she tightened, her eyes squeezed shut, her head tossed from side to side, her hot sheath clenching around him and he let go, the flood of fire rising from deep inside him, shooting up into her, pumping, pumping as he felt the release, the fountain of flames and burning ice, the intensity of his want. Again and again, he drove between her legs until he was spent. He slowed, stopped, cupped her face in his hands, and kissed her gently, forehead, eyelids, lips.

She nestled beside him on the narrow bed in the flickering room and he held her in one arm. She closed her eyes and dozed as peacefully as a child. For a moment, he felt serenity and weariness cover him like a warm quilt.

An instant later, he was fully alert, all nerves quivering. Footsteps crackled, coming their way. Before he had time to move, the doorknob rattled.

"You in there, Fargo?" It was General Avery Pearce. And he was dead drunk. "Fargo, you womanizing bastard. Where's my daughter? I know you're in there."

Devora awoke with a frightened cry as Fargo jumped up from the cot and pulled on his jeans. General Pearce beat on the door, then heaved against it. The flimsy lock snapped and the thin door flew open.

The tall white-haired figure strode in the door just as Fargo got his Colt in hand. General Pearce's huge brown eyes widened as he took in the sight of his naked daughter huddled in the cot against the wall with the blanket pulled up around her and Fargo half dressed and armed.

"Whore!" the general screamed. He fumbled and

then drew his long dress saber half out of its hilt. "Just like your mother! You whore! You—"

Before he could say another word, Fargo cold-cocked General Pearce in the temple and the tall man went down heavily and hit the floor. Fargo shut the door and blew out the lamp.

"Oh my God!" Devora sobbed in the darkness.

"Quiet," Fargo shushed her. "Your father's crazy all right. Just get dressed." As she fumbled around in the darkness donning her clothes, Fargo stood by the window and opened the shutter a crack to look out. A lone soldier came on a half run around the corner, rifle in hand, apparently attracted by the general's shouting, but he stopped short when he didn't see anyone or even a light in the line of guest quarters. The soldier walked up and down listening, then tried the handles of a few doors. Fargo waited tensely, ready to move to the door should the soldier come his way. But after a few more minutes of finding nothing, the soldier took a last look around and then disappeared around the corner.

"All clear," Fargo said. General Pearce groaned. He was coming around. In the darkness of the room, Fargo hauled the man to a sitting position. "Sorry, General," he said. He struck him again, hard at the base of the skull. That would hold him for an hour more. He made out the dim outlines of Devora now in her cape.

"Oh, Skye. I'm afraid I've got you in awful trouble. Father will probably kill you when he wakes up. What do we do now?" she whispered.

"We're getting out of here," Fargo said. "Just like I promised." He remembered the plan he'd been formulating just before Devora came knocking on his door. He couldn't very well leave her behind. And he knew damn well she wouldn't come without her father. That was going to be difficult. He thought another few minutes, pacing up and down the small room. The minutes ticked by. Then suddenly, he had it. Of course. He knelt down and checked on the general. He was out cold and would stay that way for at least an hour. It wasn't much time, but they just might make it.

"Stay here in the dark and stay quiet," he told Devora. "I'll be back soon."

She clung to him a moment and then he was off. It was a moonless night. In the faint starlight, he walked slowly and silently past the line of deserted guest quarters, turned the corner, and passed by Devora's darkened window. Some of the men were over in the mess hall and they sounded like they were having a wild party. There was one man on guard duty. A dim light burned in the general's quarters.

He passed by quietly as a shadow and found the small door to the supply house. Once inside he moved quickly. He located the shelves with the spare uniforms. He stripped down and dressed quickly in the wool trousers, boots, and long underwear of a recruit. He took a coat but didn't bother to put it on, figuring the sloppier he looked, the better he'd pass as a Fort Ravage regular, but he jammed one of the wide-brim campaign hats down over his head, which helped hide his face. He sorted through the other uniforms and found one that he thought would fit Devora, along with a hat. Then he stuffed his clothes and the extra uniform into a canvas rucksack.

The paddock was dark and deserted. He tried not to look at the loaded travois that stood there with their gruesome burdens still hitched to the horses. He saddled the pinto and led it out to stand untethered among travois. Now for the tricky part. He knew which one it was. He walked toward the travois that bore the mutilated body of Colonel Colfax covered by a blanket. It was pulled by a sway-backed sharp-ribbed roan that looked like it hadn't eaten well in a long time. None of the other horses looked any better. He hung the rucksack on the saddle, unhitched the roan and patted its nose, pulling it about gently. The travois dragged across the ground as he headed toward his quarters. Just then he heard voices. Two soldiers staggered out of the mess hall, holding on to one another and singing a song. They spotted him.

"Hey!" one of them called. "Hey! What's going on?"

The guard on top of the wall turned about to look down on him. He stopped and shrugged.

"It's Colfax," Fargo answered gruffly. "Old Shit Eye wants me to get rid of the body. Tonight. Right now."

"Pitiful bastard," one of the soldiers said with a drunken laugh as they passed by. Fargo wondered momentarily if they were referring to the general or to Colfax. The guard atop the wall turned around again, ignoring him. He continued slowly moving the travois until they were around the corner and in front of his quarters. If anyone saw the travois standing there, it would look very suspicious. He was counting on nobody happening by. There wasn't a moment to lose.

"It's me," he said softly as he opened his door. Inside he found Devora standing at the ready, fearless, her father's saber in hand. A true general's daughter, he thought. Quickly, he gave her the extra soldier's uniform and told her to dress and to cover her father with the blankets on the bed. Outside, he wrapped the blankets tightly around the still form of Colonel Colfax and hoisted him inside. In another moment, the unconscious body of General Avery Pearce lay on the travois under the blankets. Fargo secured him with the ends of the buckskin thongs on the travois poles. It might get bouncy if they had to make a dash for it. So far, so good.

Devora was ready and they walked together, side by side, toward the paddock area. Fargo crept toward the horses and brought the Ovaro to her and held it while she mounted. Normally, the pinto would buck off any rider except Fargo. But the pinto understood as Fargo patted its nose. Fargo swung onto the roan and dragging the travois, led the way toward the main gate at a slow walk. No need to draw any attention to themselves.

The guard, having heard what Fargo had said about the general wanting to be rid of Colfax's corpse, climbed heavily down the ladder, unbolted the gate, and began to swing it open. Fargo passed through and Devora was behind him until the guard called out.

"Hey, soldier. Hold on there. Isn't that Skye Fargo's horse?" Startled, Devora reined in.

"He won't mind," she said, trying to make her voice sound low. Fargo turned about to see that the guard was immediately suspicious. There was a long pause and Fargo knew Devora was trying to think what to do.

There wasn't a moment to lose. Fargo whistled and the Ovaro started forward. But the guard was too quick and managed to get the gate half shut. Fargo caught a glimpse of the Ovaro as it reared up and then heard it pounding its powerful hooves against the gate, but Devora was trapped inside.

"Go on, Fargo!" she screamed. "I'll be all right!"

"Oh hell!" he cursed. There was a groan from the back of the travois. General Pearce was waking. The jig was up. Shouts and gunfire erupted from the top of the wall. Bullets rained down. He was jolted, almost torn out of the saddle, and felt a burning fire in his left shoulder before it went numb. He was hit, he couldn't tell how bad. He cursed again. If he went back now and tried to save Devora, they would both be caught. In an instant he realized he had no choice. He had to get the general away. Then he'd return and rescue Devora. He spurred the roan forward and it pulled hard, whinnying in protest. The horse couldn't gallop dragging such a heavy weight. The best the skinny roan could do was a trot and even that would exhaust it soon.

On this moonless night, the darkness of the shadowy land soon swallowed them. From behind, he heard the pop of gunfire and shouts. The Thirteenth Mounted Infantry was getting ready to give chase. The first thing to do was to get out of rifle range from the fort. He'd dump the travois, lay a false trail, then find a hiding place. He couldn't feel a thing in his left shoulder, numbness was creeping down his arm and blood was running down his arm inside the uniform.

After a mile, Fargo reined in the roan and hopped off. He pulled off his neckerchief and using his right hand and teeth, tied it tight around his shoulder, applying pressure to the wound. The pain made his head reel. He gritted his teeth and threw the blanket off the general, who was groggy and disoriented, just coming to consciousness. He unhitched the travois and lowered it to the ground, pulled off lengths of buckskin, and bound the blankets into an aparejo he tied onto his back. He pulled the general to his feet.

"Soldier? Where are the Mexicans? Is the generalissimo flying the white flag of surrender yet? If so, then shoot them with the cannons. Blow them all up," raved General Pearce, swaying unsteadily. His mind seemed to have snapped.

"Come on, General," Fargo said. He paused and suddenly knew what to say. "The President of the United States wants to see you in Washington. He's got something important to ask you. I'm taking you there to talk to the President."

"Of course," General Pearce said. He got himself onto the back of the roan. "The President wants me to take over the country, to rule in his place. Yes, I think so. Why don't we have two horses?" he asked vaguely.

"It's safer with one," Fargo said. The left arm was completely numb now and dangled at his side, but he could tell the bleeding had stopped. In the darkness all around, there was the pop of gunfire. Fargo heard Scarbelly's shouting not too far away to his right. And on the left he spotted a movement of riders crossing the sage.

"The Mexicans!" the general said. "They're all around us!"

"Keep quiet, General. I'll get us out of here," said Fargo.

"That's a good soldier." The general clapped him on the shoulder—his left shoulder—and a wrenching pain shot through him. He felt a fresh gush of hot blood pour out of the wound. Hell, nothing was going right.

Even without the travois, the roan was having a tough time of it. General Pearce was a tall muscular man and there were two of them. The roan was undernourished and had been mistreated. Fargo patted the horse's neck, trying to encourage it. The horse broke into a sweat and tried to canter, but didn't have the strength. Fargo headed in a straight line away from the fort. In the darkness, only speed counted. With every passing mile, they had a better chance of losing Scarbelly and his men, who seemed to be charging around in circles.

After about a half hour the sounds of pursuit grew

faint. They were ten miles out. Time to throw them off his trail. His eyes had adjusted to the dim light of the stars. The faint reflection of a broad white alkali flat lay before them, surrounded by rocky gravel. At the edge of the alkali flat he reined in for a moment and scanned the dim horizon, spotting what he'd hoped to see. To his left were broken hills. Hard to his right, a few miles distant rose a high rocky butte. That would have to do.

Fargo brought the roan onto the alkali flat at a trot. Its hooves broke the cracked dry surface, leaving clear prints. He angled the horse off toward the left in a firm diagonal as if they were heading for the broken hills. He reached the edge of the alkali flat, where the land turned to crumbly gravel. It took a practiced tracker to follow a trail across gravel. One of the few ways you could spot a trail in gravel like this was to notice if rocks had been upturned. Rocks tended to trap any little bit of moisture underneath that rose through the cooling earth during the night. You would look for a rock that was a little darker than the rest, that was slightly cool to the touch. But an hour after dawn the morning sun would heat the rocks and dry out any faint sign of their passing. And he doubted any men in the Thirteenth Mounted Infantry had that degree of trailcraft. Hell, they lacked the discipline to even get the saddles off their horses.

Once the roan stepped off the alkali and onto the gravel, Fargo dismounted. The roan needed a relief from all the weight it was carrying anyway. Fargo started to reach for canteens to give the roan some water and then realized his Ovaro was carrying them. They were totally without water. He'd have to worry about that later. He and the general could keep going for the better part of a week without a drink, but the horse, carrying all their weight and in such poor condition, wouldn't last that long. On foot, Fargo began to lead the horse slowly all the way around the perimeter of the oval flat, heading to the opposite side toward the tall butte.

"Where are we going?" General Pearce asked. Fargo was too busy watching the land behind them to answer. He made sure that he and the horse didn't step anywhere that might leave a clear print. The gravel crackled in the night's silence. General Pearce hung out over the saddle, watching carefully. "Diversionary tactics," General Pearce said wonderingly, a few minutes later. "Brilliant, soldier, brilliant."

"Just following your orders, sir," Fargo mumbled. Damned good thing he had the uniform on, he thought. And maybe it was a blessing of some kind that the general had finally lost his mind completely. His arm was throbbing now, dangling at his side. His throat and mouth were dry as dust. No water. How would they find water? Dawn was now only a few hours away. From time to time, the faint sounds of gunfire echoed over the plain. With the coming of the light, Scarbelly and his men would widen their search. He had to find them a secure hiding place by then. And what was happening to Devora?

His thoughts were so confused and he was so intent on following the loose gravel perimeter of the alkali flat, that he suddenly looked up to find he was a little past the point nearest the butte. With a start he realized he was in bad shape. The pain in his shoulder was intense. And he was preoccupied with too many questions. That was just the time when a man could make a mistake—a fatal mistake.

Fargo paused a moment and gazed across the land woolly with sage and greasewood. The butte was about four miles distant. He looked up at the stars and saw that at a steady pace they would just make it by dawn.

General Pearce had fallen asleep and was lying across the neck of the roan. Fargo woke him and swung into the saddle in front of him and the roan started off. They had got scarcely a mile when the horse began to go short.

Another man might not have noticed the slight stutter in the horse's gait, but Fargo knew it spelled serious trouble. He reined in, got the groggy general down, and had a look at the roan's hooves. When he lifted the right foreleg, he was horrified at what he saw. Lodged under the horny lamina was a large stone. It had been there awhile, maybe for a week, and the tender hoof was swollen and infected. The weight of the two men on the roan's back had driven it in even further, until now even the stoic roan couldn't bear the pain and had started to limp.

"Shit," Fargo said. He pulled the knife from his ankle holster and flicked out the stone. The roan screamed. Fargo patted its flank to quiet it. The horse had taken a lot of abuse and yet it kept going. But it was in bad shape now. With a hoof in that condition it ought to have been rested up for a month. He measured the distance to the butte.

"Trouble with the horse?" the general asked. "Probably the Mexicans did it."

"Yeah. We'll have to walk," Fargo said. "The President will send some horses to meet us soon."

"Fine," General Pearce said, taking a deep breath. "It's a nice night for a walk."

They started off, but Fargo soon saw that the general kept wandering off and was staggering. He was leaving a trail that might be noticeable, even in the dense sage land. Fargo had no choice but to insist he get back up on the roan and he was soon asleep again, muttering curses and disjointed phrases in his dreams. The stars continued to turn overhead. The butte grew taller as they approached, rising up into the night sky. As he led the roan forward, Fargo heard the alarm of the burrowing owl as it swooped down to catch a small rodent. Few creatures could live in this harsh climate—owls, peccaries, small deer, armadillos, rattlesnakes, mountain lions, coyotes, and the occasional white-tailed prairie dogs.

They were nearly to the butte when disaster occurred. It happened quickly and without warning. The roan suddenly pitched forward and Fargo heard the sickening sound that every horseman fears, the snap of a foreleg. The roan had stepped into a prairie dog hole hidden under the sage. The horse cried out in agony and went down. General Pearce, awakened from his restless sleep, shouted and clung to its back.

As the horse hit the ground, the general rolled off it. In an instant Fargo sprang into action. He had no choice but to put the horse out of its misery. But a gunshot would be heard for miles. He pulled the knife from his ankle scabbard and with a swift, fast movement, sliced through the roan's jugular. Blood spurted out and the horse jerked once, twice, and then was still.

"The horse was a Mexican spy, wasn't it?" General Pearce said, getting to his feet. "It's a good thing you got it before it assassinated me. I'll ask the President to give you the Medal of Honor for this—"

The general raved on but Fargo scarcely listened. They were in a fine pickle now. Dawn was scarcely an hour away. And they could hardly leave the bloody body of the roan out here in the open. Come morning, it would attract hawks, which would wheel high in the sky and be seen for miles around. Then the vultures would arrive and finally Scarbelly and his men would come to investigate. Fargo swore.

There was no option but to find some way to bury the carcass. Or keep it from the large carrion birds. At least for a few hours until they could get away. But the horse was huge and the earth hard as a rock. Even if they had a shovel. There weren't enough rocks around to build a cairn, which would take hours in the best of circumstances. The best he could do was hide it. Maybe the hawks and vultures wouldn't spot it for a while.

Fargo scoured the surrounding land and began to collect dead branches. It was a helluva job one-handed. He tried to keep his mind off their impossible odds. With every passing moment they seemed to get worse. He forced his mind back to the task at hand. Branches. Right now, he had to find branches. There weren't a lot in this barren landscape. The general saw what he was up to and wordlessly joined in. God only knew what was going through the crazy man's mind as they piled the dead wood around and on top of the roan. When they'd finished, Fargo could see the eastern horizon turning pale yellow. There was still a mile to go to the base of the butte. And then a hard climb.

"Let's go, General," Fargo said. The general was fumbling in his pocket. He withdrew something and made a sudden movement, striking a match and tossing it onto the pile of sticks. The dry twigs caught flame. In a moment, the whole pile would be a blazing bonfire.

5

The tiny flame flickered in the dry twigs that covered the roan's carcass. In an instant, the dancing light spun along a piece of dry grass and a twig blazed up. Fargo threw himself forward, directly on top of the blaze, beating it with his one good hand, rolling over and over as the twigs crackled. He smelled the odor of singed hair and felt the burns on his hands and chest. Smoke rose in his nostrils and he coughed, sputtered, his eyes smarting. But the fire was out. He got to his feet.

"But the loyal Bucephalus deserves a funeral pyre," the general protested, trying to strike another match. What the hell was he talking about now? Fargo snatched the matches from the general's hand.

"The President wants to light it himself," Fargo said to humor the madman. "Let's go see the President. He's expecting you."

"Oh yes, of course," General Pearce said. Fargo led the way toward the butte. "He's up there? Do you

suppose he'll give us something to drink?" Fargo
nodded. What a helluva situation.

The land began sloping upward. They needed to
get on top, he told himself. Somewhere safe. He
needed an overview of the land. That way they could
keep an eye on where Scarbelly and his men were.
Rest up. Get the bullet out of his shoulder. And just
maybe they could spot some water. Fargo imagined
sitting on top of the butte. Below lay a long blue lake,
hidden by tall rocks. He would dive off the rocks
through the clear air, plunge into the cool shining
water, and—

Suddenly, he came back to his senses. The chances
of spotting water from the butte were pretty slim. But
better than nothing. He realized the combination of
pain and exhaustion was making him lose his concen-
tration. Get up the butte, he told himself.

In the dim light of predawn he scanned the formi-
dable rock face and spotted a possible path to the top.
They would have to climb through a boulder field,
scramble up a slope of scree, and pull themselves up a
deep ravine. Soon they were skirting boulders as
large as houses. The butte looked like it was riddled
with caves and for a moment Fargo considered taking
refuge in one, but the thought seemed to float away
beyond his grasp. They'd have to watch out for
mountain lions. The general stopped every few hundred feet and Fargo had to continually cajole him to
keep him going.

"Why don't we wait here for the President?" The

general sat down again. "Why don't you give me some water?"

"The President's expecting us," Fargo snapped. "He's waiting up there." For a moment, Fargo thought he saw a shadow of disbelief and sanity cross the general's face, but then his eyes went blank again. They continued to climb upward. Dawn came but Fargo didn't have time to look. He had to physically pull the general up the tumbled slope of scree. At the top General Pearce sat down on a rock and looked out as the sun spilled across the flatland below.

"Bring me some water," the general commanded. His formerly jovial tone had turned ugly, threatening. "I have to shoot soldiers who disobey me, you know. That's mutiny. I have the right to shoot anybody who mutinies."

"The water's just up there," said Fargo, pointing up at the ravine. It was a good thing the general was unarmed, Fargo thought. They had left his sword behind at the fort.

"Well, bring water down for me," General Pearce said peevishly. "I'll wait right here, soldier. And bring some bourbon too."

"But the President wants to give it to you himself," said Fargo, exasperated. They needed to get to the top now. His shoulder was throbbing up his neck and into his head now. Hell, he'd had enough of the crazy man. He pulled his Colt.

"Get up the ravine, General," said Fargo, steel in his voice. That seemed to rouse General Pearce. His large brown eyes widened and he began to climb.

Fargo lost track of time completely as he climbed, pulling himself upward with one arm. He lost his balance and smashed against the rocks, against his wounded shoulder, and felt the blood flow again. Finally, the blue sky opened up above them and Fargo pulled the general onto the top of the butte. The sun was midway up the eastern sky. Hours had passed. Fargo staggered to the edge of the cliff and looked out over the land.

Far below, a dust plume rose into the clear air. But it was too far away to make out the riders. As he watched, the plume approached the light oval bald spot in the land—the alkali flat. The yellow dust turned to white smoke in the air as the riders followed the clear tracks he had left across the alkali, then disappeared as they reached the gravel. He watched for a few minutes more, his eyes seeking any movement in the land. Yes, Scarbelly and the soldiers had been fooled. They were headed toward the broken hills in the distance. At least for the time being.

He turned away and found a spot of shade to one side of a large boulder. He sat down, removed the aparejo of bundled blankets from his back, unpacked the lengths of buckskin he'd taken from the travois, and slid the knife from his ankle scabbard. He cut some long strips off one of the blankets. No disinfectant. No sip of whiskey to dull the pain. Not even a mouthful of water. He rolled a bit of the blanket and put it between his teeth. It was time.

The general sat down on a rock nearby and seemed

to notice the bloodstains in Fargo's uniform for the first time.

"You took a bullet from those Mexicans, soldier," he said.

Fargo ignored him and began to rip the fabric away from the wound. It was damn hard to work on his own shoulder by reaching across with his right hand. And he had to bend his neck and could hardly get a clear view of the wound. Every movement was agony. The general sat watching, a faraway look in his eye.

Fargo prodded the wound and found the hard knot of the bullet. It had torn through part of his shoulder muscle, which would take a long time to heal. The bullet had lodged next to the bone, which seemed intact. Every time he probed, pain like red lightning shot along his nerves. His left arm felt like it was being held over roasting hot coals. This wasn't going to be easy. And how could he get it without tearing the muscle and making the damage worse?

He took up the knife in his right hand and began to cut the skin, trying to miss the muscle, trying to make a pathway for the bullet so he could pop it out. Blood gushed and a red curtain rose in front of his eyes. He blinked it away until he could see again. More cutting. He slipped and the pain came wrapping around him, a black wave came up around him and drew him down. He clamped down on the bit of blanket between his teeth, felt the knife slip from his grasp.

Then he felt it again, the bite of the knife, the indescribable agony of pressure against his shoulder, the rush of blood, his head whirling. He clamped his teeth and flailed out, realized someone else was there, blinked open his eyes just as he felt it give way, the bullet, pushed out and upward, coming out of his flesh as fresh pain shot along the numb nerves of his arm. He clamped his teeth again to keep the scream inside him, as somebody poked in the torn flesh, told himself to hold on, willed his mind to stop whirling, forced his eyes open to see the general raise bloody fingers in the air, holding the bullet.

His shoulder was a mass of fire, but somehow it was better than the numbness. He had to stop the bleeding he told himself. Bandage the wound. But he lay back against the rock and felt a pressure on the shoulder, the itch of wool, a tightening against the flesh, and he sank into blackness.

It was late afternoon when he woke, hot and sweaty, his mouth dry as dust, the pounding of a drum in his head. He felt feverish, his blood trilling in his veins. He raised his head, wondering where he was. The blue sky arched overhead, cloudless and hot. He was alone on top of a rock field. Then he remembered the general, looked down to see that his shoulder had been bandaged with the strips of blanket and tied tight with the buckskin thongs. It was a good job. The bullet sat on a flat rock, dark with his blood. Fargo forced himself to his feet and stood swaying, one hand on the boulder to steady himself. The white hot sun blazed down and the heat rose in waves. There was no one in sight. Where in hell had the general gone?

Fargo staggered around, blinking in the searing light, looking for General Pearce. He shouted but heard nothing. Then he heard a low moan and he made his way to the edge of the butte and saw the general standing on a rock ledge just below.

"Thanks for bandaging my shoulder," Fargo said.

General Pearce turned around and gazed up at him, then climbed back up to the top of the butte.

"That was a bad Mexican bullet you took there, soldier," he said. "I'm glad you're still alive. The army can use a good soldier like you." His eyes suddenly cleared and he seemed to focus on Fargo's face. "You're not really a soldier. But you should be. One of the bravest men I've ever seen. Dug that bullet out of your shoulder and you never said a word." The general's face clouded again. "But the war is lost. I'm afraid it's all over. I'm going to throw myself off this cliff now."

Before Fargo could move, the general climbed up onto a small rock and threw himself forward but was nowhere near the precipice. He landed on the jumbled rock, then rolled over on his back and looked up into the sky.

"Something dead is nearby," General Pearce said. "Maybe it's the Mexican soldiers we were hunting. Or maybe it's us."

Startled, Fargo looked up into the sky. Not far above them, two hawks lazily floated in circles. The carrion birds had spotted the corpse of the dead horse down below. Fargo gazed down at the flatland and saw that during the night animals—coyotes or mountain lions—had sniffed out the roan and in the course of feeding, moved away some of the branches. The carcass attracted the hawks and they would eventually attract Scarbelly and his men.

Fargo felt a wave of dizziness overcome him. His skin was burning hot, dry to the touch. A moment later, he was drenched in sweat and stars danced before his eyes. Now that the bullet was out of his shoulder, they would have to move on. They would have to find water or die. They would have to get away from the wheeling hawks. Maybe at sunset. Yes, when the sun slept, they would move on. Fargo walked back to the boulder and curled up in the shade. He felt the pounding in his head again, the throb of his shoulder. All he had to do was get up and dive into the cool lake. His shoulder was infected, he knew. It was making him sick, he was going out of his head with fever. At sunset, he told himself, at sunset he would have the strength to get up and move on. He held the Colt pistol in one hand. Just in case of trouble.

He was lying beside a campfire in his bedroll when the cold mist came sliding over the ground like a pale ghost's fingers reaching for him, pulling at his hand gently. Cold. The wind was whistling cold and he heard the soft whispering feet of the ghosts, of the long-dead and then a hoarse cry. He struggled up out of the blackness, saw the sharp stars overhead in the velvet night, felt the hard hands holding him, the bite of steel at his throat. His vision cleared. Over him was the face of a Paiute in full paint, eagle feathers in his hair. He felt for his Colt but it was gone.

"You die, white man. You die, devil who dares to defile our sacred ground," the Paiute whispered in the tongue like the Hopis and Commanches used. The knife blade began to bite into his neck.

"Friend," Fargo rasped in the Indian's language. The knife paused. "Friend of Paiutes," he repeated. His voice was so hoarse, he hardly recognized it as his own.

"This one speaks the People's tongue," the brave said to someone standing to one side.

"Friend of Paiutes," he said again. "I am called Skye Fargo. Many years, Alosaka named me Shadow-Walker."

"Alosaka. Alosaka." Fargo heard the name spoken as if from far away. He felt himself being lifted and held upright. In a moment, he blinked his eyes open to see before him a tall Paiute wearing the chief's beaded tunic and full paint. It had been many years, but he recognized Alosaka, the chiseled planes of his cheeks, the nobility of his prominent nose so like an eagle's beak.

"Alosaka. Old friend." Hope rose in him.

"Skye Fargo. You have changed."

Alosaka's black glittering eyes searched his face. He stepped forward and touched a finger to one of the suspenders holding up the soldier's uniform.

"White soldiers come to Paiute land. They make

treaty with the People. Then they take one sacred mountain. Make thunder. Make it hollow. They kill Paiutes. The People try to hide, stay away from soldiers. But they hunt down the People. Kill as many as they can. Many prayers we make to Great White Father. But he does not hear us. Instead, sends his son Cloud-Hair." Fargo could hardly follow Alosaka's words. But dimly he realized Alosaka must be speaking of General Pearce's white hair. "And Cloud-Hair makes more death to the People. And now—" Alosaka paused as if unable to go on. "And now old friend Fargo is soldier who kills Paiutes."

"No." Fargo said. The scene was whirling around him, Alosaka's voice fading in and out. "No, you don't understand. I am trying to help Paiutes. Get rid of bad soldiers. Stop Cloud-Hair."

"So you bring Cloud-Hair to defile sacred place? You show bad soldiers to the high place of the People?" Alosaka asked. Fargo puzzled over the words.

"What do you mean?" he said at last.

Alosaka gestured for him to follow. Fargo took a step forward but stumbled and was caught by the braves on either side of him. He was so dizzy, he could hardly walk. The butte and the Paiutes all seemed very very far away. He saw General Pearce, bound and gagged, lying on his side on the rocky ground. The general's eyes were rimmed white with fear. Fear of death. The general hated Indians. Then he felt himself being guided to the edge of the butte.

Night lay over the land. But a golden circle flickered below. Fargo peered down, saw a campfire and small figures around it. White men. Soldiers.

"You brought soldiers to defile the sacred ground," Alosaka said.

"No," he said again. He felt the darkness coming up over him like dark water. "No, believe me, Alosaka. The soldiers come to kill me. They tracked me here. I am trying to stop them, trying to stop . . ."

The golden circle of fire blinked out below him. The stars were gone too. He floated in black night.

Sharp pine. Heat and smoke. He felt the hands touch him again, the dull ache, the sharp pain in his shoulder. And the ghosts standing all around him, sometimes closer, sometimes farther away. A cool hand touched his forehead, which was on fire, and the ghosts leaned over him. He heard his voice calling out but he did not understand the words.

Sometime later, he felt how heavy his eyelids seemed. With an effort he forced them open, saw the dark shining eyes in a smooth moon face looking down on him, smiling. The smell of woodsmoke and herbs.

"Alosaka?" It was the only word he could say. The moon above him smiled again, her black eyes dancing.

"I am Nova," she said. He lay back and thought of a little girl long ago, with two black braids and chubby cheeks peeking out from behind a tree.

Time flowed like a dark river carrying him along. At times he knew he was sick, knew he hovered near death with the fever. Knew that the Paiutes had brought him to their village. Sometimes, the woman Nova raised his head and fed him sips of broth and herbed liquids. Other times, the ghosts came back and sat in a circle around him, chanting, and he heard his voice again, speaking words he did not recognize and he had dreams, terrible dreams. But slowly, time carried him along and broke into day and night and he began to notice the wickiup, the fire and the smoke rising through the hole to the sky, and Nova.

One day Fargo awoke, knew himself, knew the fever had broken, and that he had returned. He opened his eyes and saw the woman kneeling on the floor beside him. He lay on a thick pile of animal furs. Through the smoke-hole light poured in, a bright shaft in the smoky interior. He raised himself onto one elbow and winced as pain shot through him. But his head was clear.

"Slowly, go slowly," Nova said in the People's tongue. She brought him a bowl of rich meat broth and as he drank it, he felt himself hungry, empty inside, felt a slender strength pour through him. He sat up and the world tilted again. He stretched his arms and legs, aware of weakness and pain, but happy to feel anything, happy the gray death ghosts had fled back into the shadows.

"You are Nova. Alosaka's little sister," Fargo said wonderingly. He thought when he had last seen her with her long braids, years before. She was now a young woman, moon-faced and lovely. She wore a fringed dress with red and yellow beads and porcupine quills and when she moved around the room, he could see the outlines of her round but graceful figure.

"How long? How long was I—?"

"So many suns," Nova held up her two hands, all her fingers extended. Ten days he had been near death. Suddenly he thought of Devora back at Fort Ravage. And what had happened to the general? He pulled himself to his feet and almost pitched over. He was naked. Nova giggled and gave him some deerskin breeches to wear. He was weak and would have to rebuild. A few days maybe. He had to get back to Fort Ravage. What had happened to Devora?

"You must rest," Nova said sternly.

"Alosaka," Fargo insisted. "Take me to him. It is urgent. I must see Alosaka now."

Nova hesitated, then came next to him and helped him walk across the room. He emerged from the dim interior of the wickiup and stood blinking in the light. Before him was an amazing vista—the broad plain lay below. The wickiup, along with a couple dozen others, was built on the floor of a mammoth cavern whose wide mouth was open to the bright sunshine. Here and there, Paiute women were grinding corn and drying berries in the sun. They glanced at him with frank curiosity. Fargo gazed out at the wide land below and realized that the cavern was somewhere on the side of the big butte. This was the secret village of the Paiutes. He had heard of this place of retreat where the People went in times of trouble. Obviously this cavern was situated so that it could not be easily spotted from down below.

No wonder Alosaka had been enraged when Fargo showed up on top of the butte dressed as a soldier in the company of the general they called Cloud-Hair. Especially when the host of soldiers showed up at the foot of the butte. The near proximity of the troops made it likely one of them would stumble on the Paiutes' most secret retreat. Fargo wondered what had happened. And where was General Pearce? Was he still alive?

He leaned on Nova's shoulder and hobbled between the small wickiups, smiling to the Paiutes he passed. They nodded gravely back. She took him into the cool shadow of the rock overhang, toward the back of the huge cavern where stone apartments were stacked one on another, built in the ancient times. Nova led him through a low doorway and into the dark.

His eyes took a moment to adjust and then he saw a hole in the floor in front of him with a ladder protruding. Nova indicated that he should climb down and he knew it was the Paiutes' most sacred place, where the men of the tribe gathered for secret ceremonies. He gingerly lowered himself rung by rung into the hole, favoring his left arm, which had not yet healed.

A small fire lit the round room and Fargo inhaled the fragrance of tobacco and herbs. All around the walls sat the Paiutes, about two dozen men wrapped in colored blankets against the dank coolness. Their black eyes glittered in the firelight, their expressions solemn.

Alosaka sat in front of the small fire and he indicated where Fargo should sit. He obeyed and waited patiently. One thing about Indians was that they had a great respect for sacred things like time and place. Their meetings were not like white men's, all rushing and talking at one another. Instead, they waited and listened to the silence until the right time for speaking presented itself. A smoking pipe was passed around from hand to hand and made its slow way around the circle.

After a while, Fargo felt the time had come. He chose his words carefully.

"Shadow-Walker comes back from walking with the shadows. Many thanks to the People."

Several of the men nodded and a few smiled, pleased by his speech. Alosaka glanced around the circle as if taking the measure of each man. Then he spoke to the fire.

"For many moons we made sacrifices and prayers to the God of Thunder to stop helping white men make the sacred mountain hollow. And then comes the Shadow-Walker. Maybe the God of Thunder sends him. Maybe not. We cannot know the paths of the Great Ones."

"What is this hollow mountain you speak of?" Fargo asked. The words seemed dimly familiar. He remembered Alosaka saying something about it when they had met up on the top of the butte.

"The sacred place a day's ride away from the summer," Alosaka said, indicating the direction north. "Cloud-Hair's men go there and make the Thunder. And other white men are kept like beads on a string. But all the Paiutes are driven away and the sacred mountain falls."

Fargo thought hard. Alosaka must be talking about Dome Mountain. But what was this Thunder? Cannons, maybe? But why?

"I will go to see this thing," Fargo said. "It is a bad thing and I will stop it. To do this, I need a horse."

The Paiutes nodded but no one smiled.

"For the old friend, Shadow-Walker, there will be a Paiute horse. But where is the horse of Night and Day?" Alosaka asked. Fargo remembered that the last time he and the Paiute had met, years before, the Indian had tried everything to get Fargo to sell him the black-and-white Ovaro.

"At Fort Ravage," Fargo said. Alosaka looked shocked. "No, I did not trade it away. But after I see the Thunder in the Mountain, I will go to steal back my Ovaro."

"Good Horse Thief is Shadow-Walker," one of the Paiutes mumbled, paying him the ultimate compliment.

"We do not understand white men," Alosaka added. "Strange things we see them do—"

"Yes," one of the men interrupted eagerly. "Some days ago my brother Machakw and I rode past a white man who was hanging in a cage from a tree. Now why would white men do that?"

Fargo decided not to answer. How could he possibly explain that the man was himself and it was to make other white men think Paiutes had done it? He left the incident unanswered. There was a long silence as the pipe made another slow circle. The question of the general hung in the air. Everyone knew it but no one said anything.

"Cloud-Hair's spirit is gone," Alosaka said at last. "But his body stays behind. He is like an empty cave where only evil ghosts live. Soon his body will die too."

After another period of silence, Fargo realized that all the questions he had come with had been answered. He rose and an old man got up also, followed him up the ladder and into the daylight. He gestured for Fargo to follow and they walked along the stone buildings and then the old man stepped through one of the doors. Inside, Fargo saw a dim figure, white-haired, dressed in Indian buckskins, sitting in the corner on a rock, huddled against the wall as if afraid. General Avery Pearce glanced up at him, his face ravaged with insanity.

"I was wrong about my daughter. And my wife," he said suddenly. "The Mexicans are coming to get me. They are still angry. But the Paiutes are my family." He nodded to himself as if that explained everything, then he began singing to himself softly.

Fargo wondered if he could get any useful information out of the general.

"General, what did you want me to transport to Mexico City? On those burros? Remember when we talked about that? Was it something from Dome Mountain?"

General Pearce glanced up at him blankly.

"Moonlight," he said. "We will take Moonlight to the Mexicans." It was useless. They rose and left the room.

"Cloud-Hair was a great warrior for his people," the old man said. "He was our great enemy. If we had met him in battle, we would scalp him. But he flew away already. His spirit is in the Hunting Ground and it will do no good to take his scalp. So the People guard his body to the last day."

"Thank you," Fargo said. He left the old man and walked back through the village of wickiups. The sun was setting. His muscles were easily tired, he noticed, so he pushed himself to walk several times around the dwellings as darkness fell. Inside the shelter, Nova was waiting for him, stirring a pot of venison stew. She poured a bowl for him which he ate hungrily. And then another.

He lay down on the animal skins, suddenly tired. Nova bustled around the wickiup, cleaning up, glancing at him from time to time. He suddenly felt the empty space beside him on the pile of skins. He held out his hand to her and she came over, shyly. He pulled her down and wrapped his arm about her soft waist as she lay nestled beside him. Sleep came quickly.

Fargo woke feeling whole and strong, breathing in the faint sage smell of Nova's sweet skin as he nuzzled her neck. She stirred against him and her eyelashes blinked like dark butterflies. She smiled to herself, turned, and kissed him, her lips gentle and warm. She took his hand and raised it to cover her high soft breast. He slipped his hand inside the deerskin dress and felt the satiny smoothness of her skin, the fullness of her small breast.

Nova giggled and wiggled, sat up suddenly and pulled her dress up and over her head. Her dark eyes were merry in her round face. He drank in the sight of her tawny breasts with large brown aureoles, the nipples soft and indented. He pulled her down toward him, kissing her mouth, her breasts, first one and then another, as she bent over him. With one hand, he stroked her smooth dark thigh and cupped the firmness of her high round buttocks.

There was no need for words. Nova untied his deerskin breeches and pulled them off him. As he lay back on the furry skins, his cock pointed straight up. Nova laughed with delight and brushed her fingers along the shaft and down around his balls, as delicately as a butterfly. He started to roll over toward her, but she gently pushed him back, then kissed him, sinking her warm sucking all the way down his hardness, her tongue swirling and flicking. His nerves came alive and he cupped her breasts and kneaded her nipples gently between his fingers until she moaned and they hardened.

Her tongue was pure magic as she brought him to the brink, then slowed as his heat subsided, then quickened again, tighter around him until he thought he would burst. He slid his hand up her leg to find her portal, wet with wanting and he rubbed her lightly, then harder, flitting against the sweet small seed buried in the folds of her until at last she cried out and came, her hips moving helplessly against him. He wanted to be inside her and he started to rise again, but she pushed him back with a tinkling laugh and knelt above him, lowering herself around him as his long cock entered her slowly.

She was all heat and motion, sliding up and down on him as he held her buttocks, moving against him, one angle and then another. Her eyes grew even darker with desire as he felt her coming close again. He held her breasts and stroked her long rib cage. He felt the fire gathering in him, beginning to boil as he felt the release, not an explosion but a slow rising as she took him in again and again, rising and falling around him, sliding inside her firm heat, then coming like the flight of a rising bird against the sky, upward, upward. At last, they were spent. With a deep sigh, she fell forward and lay on his chest. They remained connected for a long time as he closed his eyes and let sleep take him.

He awoke later in the morning to find Nova gone. He rose, feeling the creaks and aches in his muscles and joints. His left arm was still sore but at least he could use it. He spent several minutes stretching. By the fire lay a heavy grinding stone that he lifted over his head a dozen times until the muscles could do no more. That was enough for now. He washed up and dressed, then left the wickiup.

He ran into Alosaka, who happened to be walking

by. Fargo asked to be given the clothes he and the general had been wearing. Alosaka looked puzzled but had them brought. Fargo discarded the bloody and ragged Union suit he'd worn, but salvaged the pants and boots. He tore the stars off the general's jacket and dusted off the wide-brimmed hat. Alosaka watched him as he dressed.

"Shadow-Walker is many men," the Paiute said.

"I will go now," Fargo said. Despite the lingering pains and aches and the weakness of his body, he was eager to be off. It had been ten days since he'd left Devora behind at Fort Ravage. He had planned to return immediately to rescue her. But things just hadn't worked out that way. And now he was worried. Alosaka called for a horse to be brought, a duncolored mare without a saddle. Nova appeared and saw that he was leaving. She stood to one side and pouted, her dark eyes sad. He wasn't sure exactly how he was going to do what he had to do. All he knew was he had to get going.

Alosaka led him to the top of the trail that led down to the plain. Here and there, among the rocks, his keen eyes spotted Paiute lookouts who kept watch over the precious hideout. The steep trail led down between ragged rocks and was invisible from down below. At the very base of the butte it came out in a narrow passage between two tall rock towers, impossible to find unless you knew it was there. High on one of the towers, he saw the figure of a Paiute. He waved good-bye and slid onto the bareback dun. The horse had been well cared-for and galloped on strong legs across the sage. Still, he missed the powerful Ovaro beneath him and wondered in what kind of shape he would find his trusty pinto.

On the sage plain, he passed a blackened campfire and realized it was where Scarbelly and his men had camped. Nearby, he spotted the pile of brush and the white bones of the horse, picked clean. It had slipped his mind to ask the Paiutes what had happened to the soldiers who had camped at the base of the butte. There was no sign of a fight here. He wondered what Scarbelly and his men made of the sudden disappearance of General Pearce and Fargo. How long did they search before they gave up?

In the distance, he could see where Fort Ravage lay. He let the dun take an easy pace. There was no use hurrying, since he couldn't very well sneak into the fort in the full light of day. When he came to within a few miles of Fort Ravage, he spotted a tumble of tall sandstone rocks that rose out of the land. He headed toward the spot. He would hole up for a while and keep an eye on the fort. See what was going on. He was too far for them to spot a lone horseman, but near enough that he could see any major troop movements.

In the small shade of the rock, he dismounted and poured some water into his hat for the dun from the animal stomach flask the Paiutes had given him, then drank some himself. It was high noon. He peeked out toward the fort. He remembered how General Pearce had planned to transport something down to Mexico City in a week's time. Well, it had already been ten days. He hoped the whole troop hadn't already managed to slip away and cross the border with whatever was the secret cargo. Maybe taking Devora with them. The thought made him sick and he forced himself to stop thinking it.

He waited and watched for about a half hour. And then his patience was rewarded. There was movement. Fort Ravage was not deserted. Dust was rising in the air. A large party of men was setting out. He put the wet hat back on his head, eyes never leaving the spot. With relief, he saw the men weren't heading south, but rather northeast, up toward Dome Mountain. Their path would take the column right by the sandstone rocks where he was hiding. Fargo took up a position hidden between two huge boulders and waited.

Soon he heard the faint sounds of horses on the move, of saddles and bridles creaking, hooves beating the trail, men calling to one another. He peered out to see that the party consisted of about twenty men and four wagons. From the speed they were traveling, he guessed the wagons were empty. The party passed right by the rocks, within ten feet of him. He kept his eyes open for Scarbelly, but the major wasn't among the soldiers.

Fargo waited until the wagons and the horsemen had passed by and then he suddenly rode out from between the rocks and up behind the last man in the column. The soldier never knew what hit him as Fargo knocked him out from behind and he rolled off his horse and hit the dirt. The dun ran along beside the other man's mount and Fargo jumped into its saddle, then slapped the dun on one flank. It angled off, then slowed and stood watching as the troop raced onward. He knew it would wander back to the Paiute village. He pulled his hat brim down low. It was just luck that none of the troop had happened to turn about at the wrong moment. Yeah, maybe at last his luck was turning, he thought. Just maybe.

The party rode on throughout the hot day. Each time they stopped for a rest, Fargo reined in well behind them as if keeping an eye on the rear. No one got a close look at him and so far he was undetected. As the darkness fell on the land, they were almost there.

Dome Mountain was a huge hulk of stone, a gently rounded mountain almost perfectly symmetrical and with a rounded top rather than a sharp peak. When the column of riders and wagons reached the base of the high mountain, they turned and rode along until they reached two low hills that stretched out like two arms resting on the plain. Between these arms of hills, in the lowering dusk, Fargo saw an amazing sight.

In the arms of Dome Mountain lay a whole complex of rickety wooden buildings, one of them with a tall chimney. Rows of wagons and barrels were lined up along fenced-in filled with rocks and wooden carts. Berms of castoff gravel rose everywhere. Men were scurrying around. What the hell was going on here? It looked like some kind of mining. As if in answer to his unspoken thought, he heard a sudden rumble and the earth shuddered. There was a grinding sound from the mountain and he spotted the entrance to the mine as a cloud of dust rose from it in the dim dusk.

Thunder in the mountain. Of course. In an instant, he knew what had been going on. The men of Fort Ravage were carrying out a secret mining operation. On Paiute land. And using army gunpowder to blast through the rock. All the while, the official reports from Fort Ravage said they were fighting off Paiutes, so the fort was supplied with more and more gunpowder.

He rode with the other men down into the camp. Men came swarming out to meet them. It was dark enough that Fargo could ride among them without anybody recognizing him.

The man leading the column proved to be Private Bucknell. "Okay, new orders from Major Roland! We're to load up the wagons now and move out."

"But we just set off another charge. In another week, we'll have another half ton."

"Major Roland says forget it. This is it! We're closing down the camp and going to Mexico."

A cheer went up from the men.

"Why can't I just take my share and skedaddle?" one called out. "Get on down to old Mexico on my own? Why not?"

"Yeah, I'm for that!"

Another man raised his voice in agreement.

"Quit that talk," Bucknell commanded. "We split up now and we'll all get run down and caught. You know it's true. Our only hope is to stick together. And if you desert, you don't get your papers. Signed by the general himself. Scarbelly's got them and you'll each get one when we get to Mexico. Most honorable discharge from the U.S. Army. Once we got that piece of paper, we're home free. They can't chase us down as deserters and there's not a damn thing the army can do but cuss. Just remember, it was what General Pearce planned for us, rest his soul. He wanted us paid in kind." A few men took off their hats. Fargo realized they sincerely thought the general was dead and he remembered the general's famous saying that "The worthy man is paid in kind." Well, these men were going to be paid in kind if he could help it, Fargo thought darkly.

Fargo tethered his horse with the others and was carried along by the surge of soldiers who pushed toward one of the buildings, while others brought the empty wagons around. The wide barnlike doors were thrown open and somebody lit a bonfire. The flickering light filtered into the building and Fargo saw the fruits of their labors, piles of silver bars, newly smelted. Not only were they mining the raw ore, but they were refining it. That took a lot of labor.

"All right, let's get this loaded in."

Fargo took a place in line as the bars of silver began to be handed one to another and loaded onto the wagons. The two men next to him were talking.

"So, we're finally rich."

"Right."

"What are we going to do with—with them?"

"Oh, I heard Scarbelly talking about it yesterday. He said we're supposed to herd 'em all into the mine when we close up the camp and blow it up. That way there won't be anybody around to tell the tale. All sewed up neat like, ya see." The other man chuckled appreciatively.

Fargo wondered who the men were talking about. Who were the *they* who were going to be killed? He decided to find out and he slipped out of line as if he were going to help the men with the wagons. The men closed ranks and he slipped away past the wagons, now half filled with the bars of silver, and crept along between the wooden buildings. Here and there stood guards with rifles, but he avoided them easily, slipping through the shadows.

Some distance away he heard a rumble of voices. It came from inside a building. He approached and found the wide door padlocked. A dim light shone through dusty panes of glass crossed with iron bars. The nearest guard was out of sight. Fargo rubbed on the dirty panes until a chink of glass was cleared and he could see inside.

He bent to look and had to blink several times before he could believe what he was seeing. Inside was a barren room lit by smoky torches and filled with rows of low wooden cots, army issue cots. On each sat a man either lying down or hanging his head dispiritedly. There must have been a hundred of them. Many wore tatters of military uniforms. Some of the men were Mexican, others were black, but most were white men. And they were chained together, bound by their ankles in long rows. The silver mines were being worked by slave labor.

6

Fargo could hardly believe his eyes. Inside the dilapidated shed, rows of forlorn men were chained together at the ankle. Even from here, he could tell they had been worked hard and fed badly. He realized how easy it must have been for the men of Fort Ravage to round up any straggling settler or stranger who happened through the territory. The army would ride in on the pretext of protecting them, then kidnap them and bring them here to work the mines. Whatever supplies they needed—from gunpowder to clothing to extra food—could be ordered right from the U.S. Army on General Pearce's request. And tonight the men of Fort Ravage planned to herd these men into the mine and blow them up to hide the evidence. It was diabolical.

Fargo heard two soldiers coming his way. He slid around the corner and listened.

"Yeah, we're going to blow the mine in a few minutes. So, get them up there just a few minutes before.

The charges are being laid right now—" They walked on until he could no longer hear them.

Fargo sprinted between the rickety wooden buildings, passing the rocky yards where he knew the chain gangs had spent the last year pounding rocks to gravel to make their masters rich. Inside the buildings must be smelting equipment, he thought, where they melted and refined the silver. He followed a wide gravel ramp up the side of the mountain toward the dark mouth of the mine.

There, in the dark he could see the dim figures of men unloading kegs of gunpowder from a wagon and stacking them right inside the entrance to the mine. Fargo joined in, lifting the heavy kegs with his right arm. He kept his eyes open for an opportunity. After a half hour, all the kegs were in place and someone called a halt. A soldier knelt down, affixed the fuses and then they began moving down the path to fetch the prisoners. Fargo saw his chance.

He slipped behind the empty wagon and waited until they had all gone. Hanging from the wagon was a canteen of water. He took off the top and carefully poured a splash of water on each wick, close to the keg of gunpowder. When first lit, the fuses would appear to be burning fine. But when the men ran for cover, the damp fuses would snuff out. He thought for a minute and then realized it wouldn't be good enough. If nothing blew, the men would come back to check on the charges.

He heard voices, shouting voices and the sound of whips. They were already driving the enslaved men toward the mine. There was no time to lose. Like lightning he hoisted one of the kegs, feeling his wounded shoulder complain, and carried it over behind the wagon. Two times he returned until there were three kegs with short fuses hidden in a ravine some distance from the cave entrance. There was no way to know whether the force of the alternative explosion nearby would cause a landslide that would seal the mine or if it would be big enough to fool the men. But there was no more time. Dimly in the darkness he saw a dark morass of humanity surging up the gravel slope.

Now he got to witness firsthand the cruelty of the men of Fort Ravage. This was what had been going on for the past year in secret. This was what Alosaka meant when he said he did not understand why white men kept other men like beads on a chain.

The prisoners came trudging up the hill, their chains clanking. On all sides the men of Fort Ravage drove them forward like cattle, using long, cruel bullwhips and the butts of their rifles. Fargo expected the prisoners would riot, but instead the men seemed to have lost all their spirit. They must have known something was afoot and perhaps they were being brought into the mine at such a late hour to be killed. But it seemed that none of the men had the strength left to rebel. Fargo stood to one side as they passed by into the mine.

None of the Fort Ravage men were near. He fell into step for a moment beside one of the prisoners, a tall black man with a long face.

"I'm a friend," Fargo said in a low voice. The black man looked at him wonderingly. "Pass the word. They're going to set off gunpowder. But I fixed it so the mine won't cave in. When the explosion goes off, wait one hour before you come out. The men will be gone. Get your chains off and do a forced march south to Fort Ravage."

The black man shook his head disbelieving.

"Pass the word," Fargo said. "If you make a sound after the explosion, they will come in and shoot you all. Absolute quiet."

The black man nodded grimly as he passed the stacks of gunpowder kegs, and entered the dark mine. Fargo stepped aside but heard him whisper to the man behind him.

"Get in there, get on! Get all the way down to the bottom of the mine," one of the soldiers yelled as he cracked the whip. Several of the prisoners at the very end of the line spotted the gunpowder kegs and guessed what was about to happen. They panicked and tried to turn about, but the men of Fort Ravage calmly drew pistols and fired at them. One prisoner went down, dead, another took a bullet in the leg.

"Carry him in with you," the guard shouted. The prisoners dragged the dead man, who was chained to them, into the darkness. They seemed too exhausted to fight anymore. There was a babble of echoing voices inside the mine as the prisoners marched on, deeper inside Dome Mountain.

When the voices were far away, deep inside the mine, the soldiers retreated down the hill. Once again,

Fargo ducked behind the wagon as one remained behind to light the fuses. Fargo waited until the man had touched a flame to each of the fuses and had run down the hill. Fargo hoped he'd got the fuses wet enough to put out the flame. He turned about and ran the short distance away to where the three kegs of gunpowder sat. The fuses were short and there would be little time to get away. He struck a match and touched it to them. The fuses sputtered, one, two, three. Fargo dashed around the other side of the wagon and threw himself down a short rocky slope, rolling over and over down the hillside, bruised and battered by the rocks.

The explosion came roaring, a bright lightning flash and a shattering earthquake. Stones and dirt rained out of the sky on top of him. There was the clatter of a landslide and an instant later, further down the mountain, Fargo heard the men of Fort Ravage cheering. He got to his feet and looked up the mountainside. It was hard to see in the moonless night, but he could tell the entrance to the mine was still clear. The wagon was gone, blown to smithereens, and a new slope of rock tumbled down alongside the mine. But the Fort Ravage soldiers were too far away to see clearly. And now they were running for their horses and wagons, heading back to Fort Ravage. His plan had worked.

In the darkness, he ran down the slope and melted into the crowd of men heading for their mounts. He found the horse he'd come in on and mounted. There was no time to lose now. He had to beat them back to

Fort Ravage. As the wagons pulled out, lumbering slowly under the weight of all that silver, the soldiers were shouting and jeering and congratulating themselves. Fargo cantered away, hidden by the dark. He grit his teeth at the sound of their laughter. He'd get his revenge all right. He put the horse into a high lope once he reached the open road. It wasn't the Ovaro, but he made good time and Fort Ravage came into sight an hour after midnight. All he could think of was Devora. What the hell had been happening to her for the last ten days without her father around? He hated to think about it.

The lone guard stood on the wall. Fargo brought the horse in on a slow walk around the back of the fort and next to the adobe wall. Then he stood on the saddle and reached upward, managing to grab on to the end of a wooden support with his good arm. He pulled himself upward. His left shoulder was still no good for lifting, but in another slow minute he was pulling himself up over the top of the wall. Hell, it was the easiest place to sneak into, he thought. At least on foot. Getting out with a horse was a little harder. But he had a fine idea about that.

As usual, the fort looked pretty deserted, with most of the soldiers out at Dome Mountain. He let himself down into the paddock and the horses stirred. One whinnied softly and he spotted his Ovaro. It walked over and nuzzled him. The magnificent animal hadn't been combed in more than a week and its mane was tangled, coat thick with dust, and it had lost weight. But the eyes were still bright, still spirited. It was saddled and bridled. No telling how long the saddle had been left on its back. He looped the reins over the saddle horn and looked about.

Devora's window was dark and there was no answer to his light tap. Raucous voices came from the direction of the general's quarters. He would look in on them in a few minutes. He approached the main gate and the guard hardly took notice of him as he climbed up the ladder. In another moment, the guard was out cold but propped up so it looked like he was still looking out into the darkness. Then Fargo examined the four rusted-out hinges of the gate. It was harder than he imagined to pull out the pins, but after five minutes of prying and pulling he managed it. The tall wooden gate was still firmly bolted from the inside but it was barely propped upright by the wall.

Now Fargo walked toward the general's quarters and pulled the military hat down lower to hide his face. The door was half open and he slipped inside. There was hardly any room, with soldiers jammed up against one another filling the room. Whiskey bottles were being passed man to man. He didn't want to ask what was going on, so he pressed himself against the wall and tried to make out what was happening. Then from the next room he heard Scarbelly's voice calling for quiet. It was impossible to see over the heads, but he heard Scarbelly's voice just fine.

"Dearly beloved," Scarbelly said. He hiccuped. The men laughed raucously. "We're gathered in here to join me to this here girl once and for all." With a start, Fargo realized what was occurring. But there were so many men, he could hardly move a step, much less stop the ceremony. He swore to himself and slipped out the door. He quickly ran around to the back of the general's quarters, searching for another entrance and then found a window. He glanced in and saw Devora all in white, her downcast eyes ringed with dark circles. Scarbelly was holding forth.

"Speak now or forever hold your peace," the major said. At that, Fargo drew his pistol and fired. Unexpectedly, Scarbelly staggered and the bullet whizzed by his head but took off his right ear. The major screeched with pain and surprise as Fargo jumped onto a crate and hurled himself through the glass window, shattering it in a shower of glass. The glass cut him, but it didn't matter.

Scarbelly's blood-smeared face was purple with rage when he recognized Fargo. He swung. Fargo ducked and made a grab for Devora, who was so shocked, she was expressionless. Fargo pulled her out the window. They hit the ground and rolled over once. Fargo dragged Devora to her feet and they ran around the side of the building, Fargo whistling to the Ovaro. At the sound, it reared up and sailed over the paddock fence, its powerful hooves pounding the dirt. Fargo threw Devora across the horse's saddle and vaulted upward as the pinto took off toward the main gate. He hunched over as soldiers poured out of the general's quarters and began firing. The bullets rained in around them as the pinto approached the gate. Devora cried out, fearing that there was no hope, no way to get through the gate.

"We're trapped!" she screamed just as Fargo spurred the pinto forward. It reared up and pounded its heavy hooves against the rickety gate. The wooden doors shuddered, then scraped on either side against the wall as the huge unhinged gate fell slowly outward. The soldiers in the yard were so shocked at the sight, they stopped firing for a moment. The big wooden gate fell, landed flat, and raised a cloud of dust. The Ovaro sprang forward, clattered across the wooden gate, and then galloped out into the darkness. The soldiers recovered themselves and fired wildly after them.

Two miles out from the fort, Fargo reined in and listened behind them. There was shouting, but he did not hear the sounds of pursuit. Probably, Scarbelly realized it was hopeless. He smiled to himself.

"Oh, Skye!" Devora said. "Am I dreaming? Is it really you?"

He wrapped his arms around her, nuzzled her hair, and pinched her lightly on the chin. The Ovaro sprang forward again. There was no time to lose. He had to get her to safety. And then there was more to do.

"Thank God you're alive!" Devora shouted above the pounding of the pinto's hooves. "Scarbelly said you were dead. Along with my father. He said they found your horse with a slit throat, killed by the Paiutes. And that both of you had been captured by Paiutes and put to death."

So that's what had happened, Fargo thought. Scarbelly's misunderstanding of the Paiute people had worked to Fargo's advantage.

"You're safe now," he said. She pressed back against his chest as the miles sped by beneath the horse's hooves. It was good to be back on the pinto again. The horse responded to his every move. Suddenly he remembered the little newspaper man.

"Where's Thaddeus?" he asked, fearing the worst.

"Turned tail and ran," Devora said in a disgusted voice. "The day after you and Father disappeared, Scarbelly locked me in my quarters. Through the window I heard that chicken-livered journalist telling Scarbelly that if the general had disappeared, he guessed he couldn't do his newspaper article. So he figured he'd just ride out and go home. The little bastard."

Fargo felt surprise. Well, maybe he'd given Thaddeus Fleet more credit than he deserved. It appeared that in the end he turned out to be just what he looked like at first, a wimpy New York newspaperman.

"I guess he's halfway back to New York City by now," Devora said, sounding bitter.

"Guess so," Fargo said. His thoughts were already on something else. The big butte was coming up and he angled off to the right, slowed the pinto, and approached the secret entrance to the hidden Paiute village at a walk. The Ovaro hesitated, then spotted the narrow entrance between the rocks and slowly walked inside. It shook its head, a signal to Fargo that the sensitive horse smelled the presence of people nearby. As he expected, they turned a corner and were suddenly surrounded by four Paiute braves, their bows in hand.

Devora screamed and threw up her hands.

"Friend," Fargo said. He recognized a young man, the one named Machakw who had spoken in the sacred circle and Fargo called him by name. The Paiutes recognized him and lowered their weapons.

"Fargo! We're going to be killed," Devora whispered as they continued on up the path.

"No, it's all right," he said, holding her close. She was panting with fear. A lot of folks were afraid of Indians. Especially the first time they saw them up close.

The Ovaro steadily climbed the path. Somehow the Paiutes had given advance warning and it seemed that the whole tribe had awakened to see him ride in. Devora gasped in surprise to see the huge cavern open around them and trembled when she saw the Indians standing silently in the darkness.

Fargo halted the Ovaro, swung down, and lifted Devora to the ground. Alosaka stepped out of the crowd.

"Shadow-Walker has stolen the Night-and-Day horse back," Alosaka said with a laugh. "This is good."

"She has come to see her father," Fargo said, indicating Devora.

"Father!? Father is *here*?? He's alive?" Fargo hadn't wanted to get her hopes up, not being sure if the general was still living. But Alosaka nodded his head and they climbed the path to the back of the cavern. Inside the cave, an old man—one of the medicine men—sat chanting and burning dried herbs on a small fire. He looked up when Devora entered and seemed to know who she was without being told.

"You have come at the right time," he said, pointing to the general, who lay bundled in blankets beside the fire. His snowy white hair lay scattered around him and his eyes seemed to look far away.

"Father, I'm here," Devora said softly, laying her hand on his. Fargo heard the hollow rattle in the general's throat that meant death was very near. At the sound of Devora's voice, the general blinked and his eyes sought hers. His blank expression cleared for a moment, as if sunshine broke through a cloud.

"My daughter," he rasped. Each word came slowly and was an effort. "My pride. So much pride. I was sick. Can you forgive me? My daughter . . ." His mouth suddenly went slack and his eyes, fixed on her face, went blank. The medicine man closed the lids and the old man's mouth. General Avery Pearce, one of the most famous war heroes in American history, was dead. They left Devora alone with her father and went outside. They paced up and down a few moments in silence.

"I went to see Dome Mountain. There will be no more thunder at your sacred place," Fargo said.

"You ride very fast, Shadow-Walker," Alosaka said with a smile.

"The white soldiers were taking metal from the

ground, silver metal. But they will not do this any-more. That is Paiute land."

"Treaty says that," commented Alosaka. "But treaty always lies. White man says here is treaty. Here is land. My People say we will stay on Paiute lands. But next year, white men come. Kill Paiutes. More treaty. New treaty says smaller land for my People. But new treaty lies too. More white men come."

Alosaka did not sound angry or bitter. Merely puzzled. And there was nothing Fargo could say to answer him, to explain his countrymen. Everything Alosaka said was true. The Indian lands were being taken inch by inch, mile by mile, year after year. Nobody thought it was possible, but Fargo knew that in the future the vast lands of the West would be filled just like the lands in the East.

"I need your help. The bad soldiers are taking this metal to the land in the south," Fargo said. "I need warriors, brave warriors, to help me stop them. They must not get away."

Alosaka glanced at Fargo in surprise.

"We People do not want to steal metal. We do not care for metal. The People want white soldiers to go to south. No. I say no. Paiute warriors will not go fight. Why do you ask this?"

"Because they *can't* be allowed to get away," Fargo said, the rage in him as he thought of Scarbelly getting away with piles of silver and a Most Honorable Discharge, spending the rest of his life in Mexico as a rich man. It burned him up and he felt his face aflame.

"When Paiute braves kill any white man, ten more

come," Alosaka said. "What good is killing white man when it only makes more come? I say, let them take the metal in the wagons and go away." He walked away toward the wickiups and Fargo watched him go.

Alosaka was right, of course. He was a wise leader of the Paiutes. Fargo had known Alosaka would be reluctant to get in the middle of somebody else's war. But he needed help. Devora appeared, walking down the path, her face streaked with tears.

"Thank you—" she said. Her voice broke. Fargo understood the rest of what she was unable to articulate. He put his arm around her and they walked back down toward the wickiups.

"You'll stay here with the Paiutes for a while," Fargo said. He felt Devora stiffen with fear. "I'll come back for you soon. You'll be all right." He saw Nova and called out her name. The round-faced woman in the deerskin dress came forward reluctantly, a jealous look on her face when she saw Fargo's arm around Devora. "Will you take care of Devora until I get back?" he asked. Nova hesitated, torn by conflicting emotions of envy and curiosity as she looked over the white woman, fingering her white dress. At last Nova smiled, held out her hand, and led Devora away.

The Ovaro came at his call and Fargo mounted. He didn't know what he would do next. He had to stop the shipment of silver from reaching Mexico. But how could one man stop a whole regiment of armed soldiers? He cursed silently and waved good-bye to the

Paiute villagers as the surefooted pinto started down the winding path.

Dawn was breaking when Fort Ravage came into view. He cursed at the sight of it. The gate gaped and the shabby fort was plainly deserted. He reined in and scanned the landscape all around.

Far to the south he saw the faint traces of the men of Fort Ravage with their wagon train heading south. South to the Mexican border, south to lives as rich men. And legally there was nothing the U.S. Army could do about it since General Pearce had apparently signed Most Honorable Discharges for every bastard at Fort Ravage. They were going to get away with it, clean as a whistle. Goddamn it, goddamn it.

He gritted his teeth and tried to think of a plan. He thought of the horde of ragged men who were probably even now marching toward Fort Ravage on foot, having escaped from the mine. A whole army of men, he told himself. But he knew they were in weakened physical condition and that there wasn't a hope in hell they could overcome Scarbelly's men, however undisciplined the soldiers were. And there was no way the men on foot could catch up with the wagons—and there were no horses. Damn it.

Fort Independence and General McNulty's troops were a good four days' ride. By the time he reached them and they returned, Scarbelly and his men would be across the border to safety. And there wasn't another fort nearby that could supply men. The Paiutes wouldn't help. He sighed. There was only himself in on this one, he thought.

He spurred the Ovaro and the horse galloped across the land, following the wide track of the wagons and the retreating men. In a matter of hours he'd caught up to them and was riding in their dust. The wagons were going at a good clip and the Fort Ravage men were spread out, keeping a good watch all around them, unlike the sloppy way they had guarded the fort. Clearly, when there was silver involved, they all got a lot more careful.

Fargo continued to dog them, staying several miles to their rear, sometimes seeking the high ground so he could look down over them and take measure of their progress. Something would come to him. Surely something would. The flatland gave way to long dry diagonal valleys where the mountains were smooth on one side and plunged down rocky slopes on the other. The wagons were following a wide path and Fargo saw that Scarbelly had not chosen to angle eastward, which would take them through the mountains and dangerous Apache territory and eventually to Mexico City. Instead, Scarbelly was heading gradually to the west, straight through the worst desert territory. They would get to the border quicker that way for certain. It was a good strategy.

As the red ball of sun touched down, Fargo saw the wagon train form up for the night. In army fashion, the wagons were brought into a circle and the horses penned inside. Then the men slept under or around the wagons with campfires dotting the perimeter. Keeping several miles back, Fargo rode up over a hill and then parallel to the wagon's trail. Then he dismounted and crept forward on foot, until he was lying down looking over the crest of a hill to the campsite.

He was close enough to make out individuals and he recognized many of the men. Then he spotted the big-gutted figure of Major Scarbelly, swaggering around the campsite. He was pleased to see a large white bandage wrapped around the major's head where his ear had been shot off. He watched as the major pulled open the canvas flap of a wagon and pulled out a bar of silver. The laughter floated up to him across the hillside.

Fargo counted the men. There were close to a hundred soldiers altogether. What if he could creep up every night and pick off four or five or six? And then get away fast. A few nights of that and the odds would get better. He considered the plan. Right now they didn't know he was there watching them. But as soon as he started firing, of course, they'd be on the alert and would send parties out to hunt for him. But it was better than nothing, he decided. As the night deepened and the stars blazed, Fargo crept in closer to the camp. He moved like a shadow and it took an hour to make his way down the grassy hillside. Chances were the guards would be so lax, they wouldn't spot him. But he was on his own. One man against nearly a hundred. If he made one mistake it was all over.

Finally, he found a spot behind a log. A few feet away was a stream with cutbanks about a yard high. He could shoot from behind the log and when they figured out where he was and started returning serious fire, he could creep away in the darkness and retreat up the hill. Yeah. It would feel good just to get a few of them.

Fargo lay behind the log, his eyes never leaving the scene before him. But something tugged at him. Something wasn't right. There was something in the air, in the valley that felt wrong somehow. He sniffed the air, looked up at the stars. For the life of him he couldn't figure out what it was. So he concentrated again on choosing his moment. He wanted to get Scarbelly and get him good. He waited until a moment when the fat major was talking to one of his men and three others rested beside the nearest campfire.

Fargo took aim and pulled the trigger. The shot exploded in the silent night. Scarbelly recoiled and dropped to his knees, then dragged himself away under the wagon. He was hit bad. Instantly, Fargo shifted his aim and plugged the other soldier, then fired off shots at the three near the fire, missing only one, who managed to dive for cover. The rest of the men came running and he struck one more, then reloaded as bullets poured over him. Fargo rolled backward and dropped between the cutbanks then ran, hunched over until he was away from the spot. He pulled himself out and began to run up the hill. Suddenly he stopped, confused. Damn it, Scarbelly and his men had outwitted him. Pouring down the slope came the soldiers, rifles at the ready. They had crept up behind him and he was caught between them like a rat in a trap. He swore, looking all around for cover. He started to retreat down the hill when he noticed that the soldiers descending the hill were firing over him, firing into Scarbelly's camp. What the hell was going on?

Fargo hit the dirt as a hail of bullets from down below flew in around him. He rolled toward a rock that provided a little cover. A soldier suddenly dove in beside him.

"You Fargo?" the man panted, firing down at the wagons.

"Hell yes. Who are you?" he asked.

"Eighth Infantry out of Fort Independence. Under General McNulty." Fargo felt the surprise wash over him.

"Is McNulty here?"

"Yes, sir," the soldier answered, reloading his rifle. "He's just up the hill directing the assault."

"I'll be damned," Fargo said. The soldier stared at him for a moment and seemed to want to ask something.

"Is—is General Pearce down there, sir?"

"No. Died last night," Fargo said.

"Thank you, sir!" The soldier sounded relieved not to be shooting at the famous general, no matter what he'd done. The soldier continued firing down at the wagons. McNulty's troops had the situation well in hand. Some of Scarbelly's men were already waving a white flag. Sporadic gunfire erupted across the landscape. But the battle was basically won. Fargo rose and ran up the hill at a crouch. He found the general standing in a knot of his senior officers.

"Fargo!" McNulty practically shouted when he spotted him. "I'm glad to see you. I thought it might be you down there in the dark. What other man would be crazy enough to take on a hundred soldiers single-handed?"

"I'm glad to see you too, General. You got here just in time."

"Thanks to Mr. Fleet," McNulty said. Fargo spotted the short journalist who edged forward. "When Colfax was murdered and you and the general disappeared, Fleet decided he knew enough to call in the troops. He got on his horse and rode out to find us. Good thing he did too."

"Well done, Fleet," Fargo said. So he hadn't been wrong about the newspaperman. Beneath that modest exterior was a clever mind and the journalist had put two and two together.

"Where's the general?" McNulty asked. When Fargo told them of General Pearce's death, McNulty looked relieved. "I wasn't looking forward to the court martial. Of course, putting him away in a lunatic asylum would have been even worse." Fargo agreed. They stood on the hill and watched the soldiers round up Scarbelly's men. In the darkness Fargo saw the large form of a man lying under a wagon. Even at this distance he knew it was Scarbelly. And he knew his bullet had killed the man. Slowly. He deserved no better.

"What's in the wagons?" McNulty asked.

Fargo told the general all about the mines at Dome Mountain and the pitiful men who had been captured and enslaved. McNulty gave orders for a detail of men well supplied with food and water to ride north immediately to intercept them.

"The way I figure it," Fargo said, "that silver belongs to those men. The Paiutes don't want it. And if the army takes it, it would look bad."

Thaddeus Fleet stood listening to every word Fargo said.

"I see your point," McNulty answered slowly. "Yes, that's exactly what we'll do. Make recompense to the poor wretches who mined that stuff."

Fargo stood looking down at the circle of wagons, the dim figures of men lining up with their hands over their heads and others moving them along with their rifles. General McNulty began walking down the hill to take a closer look.

"Aren't you going down?" Thaddeus Fleet asked.

"I've seen enough," Fargo said. "I've seen enough for a lifetime."

Thaddeus Fleet gazed down at the ruined campsite as he spoke.

"You're an interesting man, Mr. Fargo. The more I hear about you, the more I think our readers in the East might want to know more about your exploits. You know, you and I could do some good interviews together. You could tell me all about the silver mines at Dome Mountain for starters. And about General Pearce's death. But actually, I'd really like to know more about you. I mean, just how did you get started in this Trailsman work in the first place?"

Thaddeus Fleet glanced toward Fargo. But there was no one there. Startled, Thaddeus jumped and looked around him. The hillside was deserted. All of McNulty's men were gathered down below. From over the crest of the hill, Thaddeus heard the pounding of hooves. He dashed up the slope and spotted a lone rider on a black-and-white horse, galloping away across the wide land under the stars. He started to call his name, but knew it wouldn't do any good. Thaddeus Fleet stood for a long time until the rider disappeared into the night.

LOOKING FORWARD!
The following is the opening
section from the next novel in the exciting
Trailsman series from Signet:

THE TRAILSMAN #196
KANSAS CARNAGE

*1860, near the Smokey Hills of the Kansas Territory,
where old ambitions are given new meaning by
a deadly game of deceit and dishonor that threatens
to set the great prairies on fire . . .*

It was a lesson he had learned long ago. He hadn't
forgotten it, just not paid enough attention to it. But
the morning made him remember. In a single, heart-
wrenching moment, it made him remember.

The morning sounds were always wonderful har-
bingers, the voices of the songbirds, the black-capped
chickadee, the horned lark and the redwing, the busy,
scurrying sounds of the fox squirrels, prairie dogs and
gophers, all offering comfort. The morning smells
were next, the ever new scent of the dew-wet grass,
the special, rich odor of the soil waking to the sun, the
full, slightly sweet aroma of the black walnut seeds.
These odors, like the sounds, could make the morning
a warm and welcoming embrace.

But the morning sounds and smells were not
enough. There was a third element. It took the harsh-

ness of seeing to make the morning complete, the un-
forgiving reality of everything given shape and form,
sounds and smells made real. It had happened before,
and now it happened again. He had wakened,
washed in the brook, was almost finished dressing
when the column of smoke rose from the horizon, just
over the distant hills. A sudden, silent intrusion that
spiraled upward, piercing the sweetness of the morning as a dagger pierces a cloak. Skye Fargo's lake blue
eyes narrowed as he saw the column of smoke rise
into the air. To the Trailsman, a column of smoke was
not simply a column of smoke. Like every other sign,
print, mark, and trail, it spoke in its own way, with its
own voice. Campfire smoke was erratic and fitful and
came apart in the air. Smoke from a brush fire was
stringy and spread quickly. Smoke from a burning
wagon was white to gray-white. Smoke from a burning house was thick and dark gray to black.

Fargo felt a curse catch in his throat as he watched
the column of smoke grow thicker and blacker. He
was buckling on his gun belt as he raced across the
ground to where the Ovaro grazed in a patch of
downy bromegrass. Flinging the saddle over the pure
white back of the horse, he yanked the cinch tight and
vaulted onto the horse. In moments the Ovaro was
galloping toward the hills, its jet black fore and hind
quarters glistening in the morning sun. He sent the
horse in a direct line toward the column of smoke,
and when he began to descend over the last low hill,
he turned right into a stand of bur oak. The land flat-

tened out as he neared the bottom of the hill, became more open, but Fargo stayed inside the trees.

He heard high-pitched shouts and whoops before the house came into sight, burning fiercely, the thick black column of smoke still rising from it. He was actually glad to see the nearly naked horsemen on their short-legged Indian ponies racing back and forth. It meant their grim business was still unfinished, and he saw the reason why as they poured arrows into a small, flat-roofed, solid stone structure a dozen yards from the burning house. The family, at least all those left alive, had taken refuge in their cold-storage house built to keep grain and other perishables away from the rodent population. Fargo drew the pinto to a halt, reached back, and pulled the big Henry from its saddle case. He took a quick count as he brought the rifle to his shoulder, came up with ten or twelve racing horsemen. Staying in the trees, he fired two shots and saw two of the attackers fly from their ponies. Another figure crossed in front of his gunsight, and he fired again. The Indian toppled sideways from his pony, and Fargo saw the others begin to peel away in two directions.

They wheeled, half circled in surprise and alarm. Fargo held his fire. The Indian didn't like surprises. He liked being trapped even less. But most of all, he disliked an unknown enemy, who they were, how many, if there were more on the way. They peered into the trees as they backed and circled, but they still hesitated. Fargo moved the pinto sideways some dozen feet, fired again, moved sideways again and fired. One of the attackers pitched to the ground. It was enough for the others. Unsure how many attackers were in the trees, they decided on retreat. One, a young buck, wheeled his pony in a tight circle as he brought his arm down in a short, chopping motion, and the others followed him as he raced away.

Fargo peered at the fleeing riders, focused on the armband of one. "Pawnee," he muttered as he saw the distinctive decorative patterns that the Pawnee favored. He stayed in the trees, listened until he was satisfied that they were gone, and slowly nosed the Ovaro out of the oaks. He rode to the stone storehouse and had dismounted before the door opened. A man stepped out, his face tight with fear and strain, an old Hawkens plains rifle in his hands as he stared at Fargo.

"Just you, mister?" he said.

"Just me," Fargo said.

"Jesus, from the way they were dropping I thought there were at least half-a-dozen of you," the man said.

"That's what they decided." Fargo smiled, and the door opened wider to reveal a woman and two small boys. Fargo's glance went over the four of them. "Anybody else?" he asked.

"No, just us. We were lucky. We saw them coming and got in here in time," the man said. "But they'd have gotten to us sooner or later if you hadn't come by. We'll be owing you forever, mister. I'm Jed Harrison and this is my wife, Martha, my boys, Ted and Terence."

"Fargo, Skye Fargo," the Trailsman said.

"I'm worried about the Beeneys," Martha Harrison said, stepped from the stone storage house. "They live a mile north. Those stinking savages came at us from the north."

"I'll go see," Fargo said. "Meanwhile, you stay here in your storage house. It's the best place for you until I find out more."

"You think they'll be coming back?" Jed Harrison asked.

"No, but you can't ever be sure about Indians. You stay holed up here. I'll be back," Fargo said, and pulled himself onto the horse. He waited till the Harrisons retreated back into the storage house and closed the door before he rode away. His path followed the Pawnee tracks north until they turned and rode west. They hadn't slowed, their prints still digging deep into the ground, he saw, and felt relief for that much. But the relief didn't last, ending as he crested a low rise and came onto the Beeney house. What was left of the Beeney house, he corrected himself, a blackened pile of still smoldering logs. Outside lay the bodies of a man, a woman, and three children. He halted, swung to the ground, and went from one form to the other, hoping to find life still clinging to someone. But he found only brutal death. Terrible things had been done to the woman before she was killed. The man, too. And the oldest of the children, a young girl. They were the kind of things that marked fury and rage.

When he walked back to his horse, the frown dug deeply into his brow. He knew the Pawnee. Like most of the warrior plains tribes, they were savage fighters and clever, resourceful attackers. They could be fierce and cruel, giving no quarter and asking none. This was their way, the warrior's way. But what he saw here had a different feel to it, a stamp of viciousness that was beyond the Pawnee way. More than fighting back, it bore the stamp of retaliation. The frown stayed with him as he climbed onto the Ovaro and rode back across the hills.

He reached the Harrisons to find the fire had burned itself down to smoldering ashes. The family came out of the storage house at once, the woman peering hard at him. "Oh, my God," she murmured, reading the set of his face. "Oh, my God. All of them?"

Fargo nodded. "Get together whatever you've left. You can't stay here," he said.

"Maybe they won't hit us again. Maybe this was just a raid. We can rebuild," Jed Harrison said.

Fargo tried to keep the impatience from his voice and knew he wasn't succeeding. "This was no ordinary raid. Get your things. We've no time to waste talking," he said, and watched as the family began to salvage what little they could, a trunk that had resisted burning, a strong box no doubt filled with family papers, some clothes that had hung on a clothesline off by itself. Jed Harrison brought out a standard utility one-horse farm wagon that had been in a wooden shed back of the trees. They loaded their few remaining possessions into it, and then the youngsters climbed in as Harrison took the reins. Fargo rode ahead a few hundred yards, surveyed the terrain, saw nothing to bother him, and fell back to ride alongside the wagon. The sight of the Beeney home stayed with him. "How many more families in these parts?" he asked.

"Just Ed and Sarah Culligan. They're south of here," Harrison said.

"We're going south. We'll stop there," Fargo said.

"I've been afraid this was coming," Martha Harrison put in.

"Why?" Fargo frowned.

"We've seen so many more of them lately, more than we ever have. They kept their distance, but they kept coming by, gave me the shivers every time," the woman said. "Where are you taking us?"

"There's a fort south of here," Fargo said.

"Army post. Fort Travis. But that's a few days' ride," Jed Harrison said. "There's no hiding place out here, Fargo."

"I'm hoping to catch sight of a platoon on patrol. They can escort you to the fort," Fargo said.

"Haven't seen any of those around in some while," the man said.

"What made you settle out this far? You're way

past what the army calls safe land," Fargo said. "Not that their safe land is so safe."

"Good land for the taking," Harrison said. "We figured the army patrols that came this far would keep things peaceable. Seems they did until lately."

Fargo turned the man's answer in his mind. Good land for the taking, he echoed silently, a dream of naïve, trusting souls and of stubborn, thick-headed fools. It didn't much matter which they were. Maybe a little of both. But it was the other things he had said that bothered Fargo. Things had been peaceable, and now suddenly they were not. The great plains were always a tinderbox, always a place where sudden beauty and sudden death existed side by side. But what he had seen this morning with his own eyes, and heard from Jed Harrison's lips, hinted at something more, events that cast shadows. But shadows of what? he grunted. He had no idea. He knew only one thing. He didn't like it. He knew how fast a prairie fire could erupt and consume everything in its path. The fires of hate and rage could spread just as fast.

He pushed the thoughts away, and his eyes scanned the ground as he rode. There were unshod pony prints all over, too many for just hunting parties. They were approaching a dip in the land, box-elder and black oak thick across the terrain, when rifle shots erupted. "Oh, no, oh, God," Martha Harrison gasped at once. "Down there, that's the Culligan place."

"Get under your wagon and stay there," Fargo

barked as he reached back, pulled the big Henry from its case. He spurred the Ovaro forward, swerved the horse through the black oak as more rifle shots sounded. He rode hard down the incline until the land flattened and he saw the cleared area, the house and barn in the center. A half-dozen loin-cloth-garbed riders were pouring arrows into the house. Rifle fire came from two of the windows, sporadic and wide of the racing horsemen. These weren't the ones who had attacked the Harrisons, Fargo saw at once. They were all young bucks, and they lacked the experience and controlled purpose of the others, their assault more exuberant than effective. Fargo drew a bead on one as he halted the pinto and fired. The Indian flew sideways from his pony. The others turned at once, took but a split second to see the figure on the ground, and streaked away in all directions. Fargo sent a shot after them as they fled into the trees behind the house. He listened for a moment and was satisfied they were racing away.

He moved the pinto into the open, and the door of the house opened. A man, a teenage boy, and a woman came from the house, both the man and the boy holding old army carbines. "You alone, mister?" the man called out.

"Your neighbors, Jed and Martha Harrison, are back a ways," Fargo said. "You're Culligan?"

"That's right. This is Jeff Carter. He came to work for me last week," Ed Culligan said.

"I don't think I'll be staying," the boy said, his face chalk white.

"Nobody's staying," Fargo said. "Get together what you want to take. The Harrisons were wiped out. The Beeneys killed."

"Dear God," Sarah Culligan breathed.

"Same ones that just hit us?" Culligan asked.

"No, others. A lot worse," Fargo said.

"Why all of a sudden? They haven't bothered us until now," the man blurted out in exasperation.

"I always heard Indians don't need a lot of fancy reasons," the youth muttered.

He wasn't entirely wrong, Fargo grunted silently. Yet there were reasons here. He felt it inside him as he thought back to the scene at the Beeneys'. No sudden, random explosion, not this. "I'll fetch the Harrisons. Get yourselves ready to go," he said. He turned the Ovaro and rode back up the incline. The Harrisons were under their wagon when he reached them, and he gave an approving nod as they emerged. They followed him back to the Culligans, where he found a freight wagon outfitted with stake sides. Sarah Culligan sat inside it amid a welter of boxes and trunks. Culligan held the reins of a two-horse brace, and the boy, Jeff, waited astride an old roan with a graying mash.

They exchanged greetings with the Harrisons, a grim and unhappy meeting, and fell in beside each other as Fargo rode ahead. Once again he scanned the terrain and saw too many unshod hoofprints. An object on the ground caught his eye, and he halted, dismounted, and picked up a torn piece of moccasin. A frown came to his face as he examined it. It wasn't Pawnee, he saw. He stared at it for a long moment. The Pawnee made their moccasins with a double seam along the side of the sole. His lips pulled back in distaste, he pushed the piece of deerskin into the pocket of his jacket and returned to the saddle.

He wouldn't rush to conclusions, he told himself. Besides, he hadn't enough to do that. But he was growing more and more apprehensive, he admitted as he put the pinto into a trot. The land thinned out, became clusters of hackberry, and the sun moved into late afternoon. He paused occasionally at a high place to let the wagons see him before riding on again. The day was beginning to draw to a close when he saw a movement of branches along a stand of hackberry. They moved in a straight, steady line, and he sent the Ovaro forward. Blue-clad uniforms appeared and began to turn to go back the way they had come. Fargo shouted as he spurred the horse on and frowned as he saw but six troopers, an officer at the head of the group.

The officer saw him and drew to a halt as Fargo rode up. "You're riding hard, mister," the officer said, a lieutenant's bar on his shoulder. Fargo took in the young, earnest face, blond hair reaching down beneath his cap, and a small blond mustache that was unable to add maturity to his unlined face.

"Trouble," Fargo said. "Two families are following me. A third didn't live to run."

"Indian attacks?" the lieutenant said, his face tightening.

Fargo nodded. "Been looking to find a patrol. Where's the rest of your platoon?"

"There is none. This is it. I'm Lieutenant Roswall."

"A six-man platoon?" Fargo asked incredulously.

"That's right," the lieutenant said.

"That's crazy," Fargo blurted. "Who the hell ordered that?"

"General Cogwell at Fort Travis," Lieutenant Roswall said, keeping his voice flat.

"A six-man platoon's like the tits on a bull, not good for anything," Fargo said.

"We've orders only to reconnoiter. We're supposed to avoid engaging the Indians," the lieutenant said.

"What if they engage you?" Fargo snapped.

"We run," Lieutenant Roswall said grimly.

"If you can," Fargo grunted. "This is the damned stupidest thing I ever heard."

"Generals decide field policy, not lieutenants," Roswall said. "I was about to turn back. I've come out farther than I'm supposed to go."

Fargo was still shaking his head in wonder as the two wagons rolled into view. "I was looking for an escort to get these people to the fort," he said.

"We'll take them," the officer said.

Fargo snorted. "Hell of a piss-poor escort," he said. "Nothing personal."

The lieutenant shrugged. "Sorry, can't do any better," he said, and Fargo heard the apology in his voice.

"No, you can't. Guess I'll ride along with you. I'll be one more gun in case they decide to jump us," Fargo said.

"Let's hope they don't," Lieutenant Roswall said. "There haven't been any raids near the fort."

"Guess the trouble's back north across the plains," Fargo said. He brought the Ovaro alongside the lieutenant as the rest of the troopers flanked the two wagons. The little procession moved south, staying near the hackberry, and Fargo still felt the anger pushing at him.

"Why the reconnaissance patrols?" he asked the lieutenant.

"Guess General Cogwell wants to know what's going on anywhere near the fort," Roswall said.

"He could send out scouts to do that," Fargo said. "If he sends out a platoon, it ought to be able to take care of itself, at least."

"The general's keeping most of the troops in and around the fort," Roswall said.

"Why? He expecting trouble?" Fargo queried.

"I asked that," the lieutenant answered. "He said no. He just wanted a strong deterrent force at the fort just in case."

Fargo snorted and decided to drop the matter. As the day came to an end, they made camp alongside the hackberry. Fargo took awhile before he could sleep, the events of the day still clinging, not so much for themselves but for what they might mean. But finally he slept, and in the morning they resumed the journey after sharing army breakfast rations. They made better time than he expected, and it was still light as they neared Fort Travis.

Settlers' houses began to appear, spread out with plenty of farmland between them. The road wound through the new homes, which grew more plentiful as they neared the fort. Fargo saw the fort itself come into sight, took in a good enough stockade fence but no corner blockhouses. Sturdy enough, yet no major fort such as Pitt or Laramie. He saw the stables and barracks were contained inside the stockade walls. He also saw a line of army tents outside the stockade. The general was definitely taking precautions, unusual ones for someone who didn't expect trouble. As troopers escorted the Harrisons and Culligans inside the fort, Lieutenant Roswall paused beside Fargo. "Come along while I report to the general," he said.

"Fine," Fargo said, and followed the young officer into the separate building that was the general's quarters. He waited as the lieutenant made his report. When he was called, Fargo stepped into the inner office. "This is the man who saved two of the families," Roswall introduced.

"Skye Fargo," the Trailsman said. His glance took in a tall man in a sharply pressed uniform, graying hair atop a face that was coldly handsome, with a stiff, unbending quality to it. General Cogwell had a well-built frame, a trim body, and blue eyes that were as cold as they were piercing. His thin lips had difficulty offering a smile that was not sardonic.

"Skye Fargo, I know that name," General Cogwell said, peering at Fargo as his lips pursed. "I make a point of remembering names. Give me a few moments."

"You make a point of small platoons," Fargo said.

General Cogwell returned a tolerant smile. "You disapprove?" he said.

"Can't understand why," Fargo said. "You've plenty of troops here at the fort."

"Precautions. I believe in precautions."

"Seems to me like you're expecting trouble."

"I certainly hope not. But I'm not charged with keeping the territory peaceful, just protecting Fort Travis," the general said. "General Miles Davis is in charge of keeping peace." He stopped, snapped his fingers loudly. "That's it, Fargo. You're an old friend of Miles Davis. You've worked for him, scouted for him."

"That's right," Fargo said. "You keep track of things."

"I make it my business to. You see General Davis lately, Fargo?" Cogwell asked.

"No, not in a while," Fargo answered.

"It's his job to keep peace in the territory, you know. I just hope he's doing the job he's supposed to be doing," Cogwell said.

"I know Miles Davis. I'm sure he is," Fargo said.

General Cogwell's smile was laced with condescension. "The two families you brought might not agree with you," he said.

"Perhaps not," Fargo had to concede. "Makes me real curious as to what's going on. Maybe I'll pay General Davis a visit."

Cogwell's voice grew cold. "I consider that entirely unnecessary, actually, quite useless," he said, and Fargo's irritation rose at the man's tone.

"I consider six-man platoons pretty damn useless," Fargo said, and saw the general's face stiffen.

"I decide what's appropriate around here," Cogwell said.

"And I decide who I'll visit," Fargo returned.

"You may show Mr. Fargo out, Lieutenant," Cogwell said.

"It's been a real pleasure," Fargo said as he walked from the office with the lieutenant at his side. Outside, Roswall offered an apologetic shrug.

"The general can be difficult to deal with," the young officer said.

"Me, too." Fargo smiled, pulled himself onto the Ovaro, and swept the inside of the fort with a long glance. "What'll he do with the two families?" Fargo asked.

"Put them up, maybe with some of the other families for now," Roswall said.

"Thanks for getting them here," Fargo said.

"Glad I could help," the lieutenant said.

"If General Davis is in charge of keeping peace in

the territory, he's got to be set up somewhere on the plains. You know where, Lieutenant?" Fargo asked.

"He's set up a field camp along the Smokey Hill River," Roswall said. "Smack in the middle of Pawnee country."

"That'd be Miles Davis," Fargo chuckled. "Let the enemy see you're not afraid. Much obliged, Lieutenant. Good luck."

"Same to you, Fargo," Roswall said.

Fargo moved the pinto through the fort at a walk, out through the houses that stretched outside the fort. He paused to glance at the line of army pup tents that ran outside the stockade walls. It was a strange, almost incongruous scene, Fargo decided. General Cogwell was plainly very concerned about the safety of the fort and the community that stretched out beyond it. He had a heavy complement of troops inside the fort and extra soldiers set up outside. Why was he so big on precautions yet willing to send out six-man platoons that weren't much use for anything except targets?

It made no sense, as unexplainable as the eruption of hate and rage he had seen yesterday morning, Fargo pondered. He was still seeking some reason when the sun descended and he found a spot to bed down in a thicket of black oak. But he'd decided one thing. He'd definitely pay Miles Davis a visit. It had been a long time since he'd seen the general, and he had one more reason now. It wasn't often he was close enough for a visit. But as he settled down on his bedroll, he knew one more thing. He'd not be riding with casual ease. Something was brewing on the Kansas prairie. He felt its long, grim shadow as he finally slept.

**A SWEEPING NOVEL OF THE
ALASKAN FRONTIER—A FROZEN WILDERNESS
WHERE A MAN COULD FIND HIS LIFE,
OR LOSE IT . . .**

LOUIS L'AMOUR'S

SITKA

He was born in the swamps of the Eastern States, and came of age on the frontier. An adventurer, a sailor, and a man who knew where he was going, Jean LaBarge found a challenge he would live and die for—on the rugged coast of the Alaska Territory.   (194012—$5.99)

Prices slightly higher in Canada.